DUEL

☆

"Shall we get on with it?" asked Hadley, sounding bored rather than anxious. "I'd like to be home in time for breakfast."

Torn felt his face get hot. He smiled thinly. "You'll get home, Hadley. But you'll be in no condition to eat."

"Gentlemen, are you ready?" called Hugh Reklaw.

They said they were.

"Begin. One. Two. Three . . . "

Torn was amazed at how acute his senses had become. He could almost taste the air he breathed. He could hear the crush of wet grass beneath his boots.

"Seven. Eight. Nine . . . "

An icy calm overwhelmed him.

"Ten!"

He pivoted on his heel. Hadley was also turning. He seemed a long way off. But when Hadley's pistol came up, the distance closed so swiftly that it made Torn dizzy. He lifted his own arm, drew a bead, and caught his breath as white powdersmoke obliterated from his view the pistol in Hadley's hand. Torn heard a soft *thump!* An invisible fist knocked him off balance. He gazed at a spreading stain of crimson on the front of his white shirt.

Also by Hank Edwards

THE JUDGE

WAR CLOUDS

GUN GLORY

TEXAS FEUD

STEEL JUSTICE

Published by
HARPERPAPERBACKS

HANK EDWARDS

THE JUDGE

LAWLESS LAND

HarperPaperbacks
A Division of HarperCollinsPublishers

HarperPaperbacks *A Division of* HarperCollins*Publishers*
10 East 53rd Street, New York, N.Y. 10022

Cover illustration by Mike Wimmer

First printing: January 1992

Printed in the United States of America

HarperPaperbacks and colophon are trademarks of
HarperCollins*Publishers*

10 9 8 7 6 5 4 3 2 1

C H A P T E R

1

IT WAS LATE AT NIGHT WHEN CLAY TORN reached the sleeping town of Warrensburg, Missouri. A tall man on a tall horse, he veered off the road from Springfield at the outskirts of the Johnson County seat. He passed a small frame house. The night was bitter cold, and he looked longingly at the warm amber lamplight gleaming in the windows.

A coating of snow rode on the broad shoulders of his black greatcoat. Chilled to the bone, he shifted uncomfortably in the wet saddle. A relentless, gnawing ache in his thigh plagued him. Old war wound; a fragment of a minié ball was still lodged there, and reminded him of its presence every time the mercury plummeted.

A hound squirmed from under the porch of the house and howled at him. Startled by the clamor, his

1

horse snorted, blowing vapor. Torn calmed the dun gelding with a few soft-spoken words and steered the animal into a wider loop around the house.

Passing through an open gate, he quartered across a pasture blanketed with the snow that had been falling for most of the previous day. Ahead stood a black line of trees. Beyond it, he knew, lay the tracks of the Pacific Railroad, a ribbon of iron cutting east-west across Missouri's midsection, linking St. Louis and Kansas City.

The snow, pastern high, crunched beneath the dun's hooves. The impenetrable layer of clouds that had blocked the sun all day was now breaking apart, revealing a silver moon. A blustery north wind cut into Torn's eyes and made them water. A woolen scarf helped some, covering the lower half of his face and tucked securely beneath the upturned collar of his greatcoat. He managed to keep the tip of his nose reasonably warm with his own breath. The clearing sky promised below-zero temperatures before dawn.

He realized that anyone who chanced to see him now—a lone rider, his face covered, in the dark of night—would probably take him for an outlaw and be fully justified in the assumption. Missouri had more than its share of desperadoes.

Clay Torn was no outlaw. He had been once, at the close of the war almost a decade before. A long time ago, but the memories of those months as a wanted man, hunted with a fury by the entire United States Army, were indelibly etched in his mind. Not good memories, those.

Now he was a federal judge. It struck him funny

how life could take so many wholly unexpected turns.

He'd been born and raised on a South Carolina plantation, Ravenoak, to one of the oldest, most illustrious families in the Palmetto State. Blue-blooded southern aristocracy. The war had cut short his study of the law—every family had felt the need for a lawyer in those troubling times. After going off to fight for the Cause, he'd been captured at Gettysburg, and he had languished in a federal prisoner-of-war camp until the close of the conflict.

After killing a sadistic guard and escaping that hell-hole, he'd returned home to find Ravenoak devastated, his family killed, and his fiancée abducted by Yankee deserters—some of Sherman's blue-coated wolves.

He'd headed west to search for Melony Hancock, his one true love, and in turn had been searched for by Union soldiers with orders to shoot on sight.

He was no longer hunted, but he was still hunting. Ten years of false leads and cold trails lay behind him, and still no Melony.

But she was still alive. Somehow he knew. His heart told him. And now he glanced pensively at the lights of Warrensburg, wondering if by chance Melony was in one of those houses, or in Missouri, or a thousand miles away. As he so often did, he wondered, too, what she was doing at this very moment and if she wondered the same about him, or thought about him at all anymore.

Guiding his horse through the windbreak of trees, he saw the Pullman palace car through a web of dormant, sapless branches. Skeleton limbs clacked together, sounding like a thousand telegraph keys going all at once.

The Pullman was parked on a side track at the rim of the Warrensburg rail yard. Torn could smell woodsmoke; the stiff north wind bent a ribbon of black smoke into the trees where he paused. The smoke issued from a stovepipe jutting from the roof of the Pullman. The smell of a warm fire made Torn colder still.

The palace car stood alone. Storm lanterns illumined the platforms fore and aft. Torn saw no one. Heavy drapes were drawn over the Pullman's windows. The car bore no identifying marks. But he was sure this was his destination.

The attorney general of the United States was supposed to be waiting for him inside the Pullman.

Slight pressure from Torn's knees got the dun moving again. Wouldn't do to keep the boss waiting.

Reaching the Pullman, Torn dismounted stiffly. His feet were blocks of ice. As he hitched the horse to the platform railing, a stocky man in a red plaid mackinaw coat emerged from the car.

"Judge Torn?"

"That's right," said Torn, teeth clenched to keep them from chattering. "Who are you?"

"Frank Havelock, U.S. marshal."

He proffered a blunt-fingered hand. His grip was firm, the handshake vigorous. Torn didn't take off his glove. It would have been the gentlemanly thing to do—he knew all about how gentlemen were supposed to conduct themselves. He'd been one—once.

But it was just too damn cold for worrying about protocol.

"Come inside," invited Havelock. "It's cold as a banker's heart out here."

"Can't leave my horse long without shelter."

"I'll see to that directly."

The marshal was crisp, businesslike, his eyes black bullets beneath a stern brow. A sweeping mustache screened his mouth and framed a massive jaw. The mackinaw coat bulged at the hip—he was "heeled" and had the look of a man who'd cut his teeth on a gun barrel.

Torn mounted the platform and stepped inside. The Pullman was positively torrid, and he breathed a sigh of vast relief as the warmth enveloped him.

"Ride all day?" asked Havelock, coming in behind him, shutting the door quickly. "Reckon you've forgotten what it is to be warm. Like some brandy?"

The marshal moved to a sideboard, where crystal decanters stood on a tray of scrolled silver.

"Brandy will do nicely, thanks."

Torn gazed in wonder at the opulence of the private car—Turkish carpet, Venetian crystal chandeliers, mahogany chairs and settees upholstered in burgundy velvet, satinwood and gold-leaf embellishments. Dark green velveteen adorned with gold cord draped the windows. A fire popped and crackled cheerily in a big black iron wood-burner.

"Mighty fancy, isn't it?" Havelock smiled. "Puts me in mind of a bordello I've been to in St. Louis." He carried a glass of brandy to Torn. "Here you go. Beats the bust-head you usually get out here. Won't eat rust off metal, but I guarantee it will stoke a gut fire."

A man entered from an adjacent room.

"Drink up, Clay," urged the attorney general of the United States. "You'll need a good stiff drink under your belt when I tell you about the job I have in mind for you."

C H A P T E R

2

ATTORNEY GENERAL GEORGE WILLIAMS WAS A tall, gaunt individual, and his blue broadcloth suit hung like a sack on his lanky frame. He crossed the room with long, loose strides. As they shook hands cordially, it struck Torn—as it did every time he laid eyes on this ungainly yet dignified gentleman—that Williams bore a slight resemblance to Abraham Lincoln. The attorney general was a forceful personality, with an air of probity and vast wisdom about him. He was a man both honest and cagey.

"Thanks for getting here on such short notice," said Williams. "I'll take one of those, Marshal, if you don't mind."

While Havelock poured another brandy, Torn shed his greatcoat and gloves. He stowed the latter in a pocket of the former and hung the coat on a brass hook near the door to the platform.

Havelock delivered a glass to Williams, who raised it in a toast.

"To that rarest of all commodities—particularly, it seems, here in Missouri—law and order."

They drank to that.

Havelock hadn't shucked his mackinaw coat, and when he'd finished fortifying himself, announced that he would see to Torn's horse. Williams nodded, and Torn sensed that Havelock's departure at this stage of the parley had been prearranged.

The marshal gone, Williams settled in a wing chair and motioned for Torn to take a seat in another.

"I have a difficult task in mind for you, Clay. But first I wanted to speak privately, to talk a moment about the war."

Torn's gray eyes were as bleak as the wind that rocked the Pullman with its battering gusts.

"We all lost something, someone, in that terrible conflict," continued Williams gravely. He turned the brandy glass in his hands, gazing soberly at the swirling liquor. "Some of us more than others. I know you lost everything. A tragic turn of events."

"What's done is done."

"Indeed. Doesn't do much good to cry over spilt milk. But circumstances can embitter a man. Are you bitter, Clay? Do you still fight the war?"

"No."

"Others do. Here in Missouri, lawlessness is rampant. Many of the outlaws are ex-guerrillas who to this day have refused to take the loyalty oath or who took it never intending to abide by it. Some roam in small gangs; others operate in what amount to small armies. A lot of the citizens aid and abet them. A large proportion of these bandits once wore Confederate gray. Were, at one time, your compatriots."

"I think I see what you're getting at," said Torn. "The war is over. These men you speak of have no honor. They are not compatriots of mine. They may claim they're still fighting for the Cause, but that's just an excuse for outlawry."

Williams nodded. "I was confident you felt that way."

Despite the man's genial approach to the subject, Torn was nettled. He decided to prod the attorney general.

"I'm right surprised," he said, laying on a southern drawl just for effect, "by this line of questioning. I thought you knew me better. And I thought I knew you better."

Williams held up a hand, fingers splayed. "Don't take offense, Clay, please. Loyalty is a ticklish subject here in Missouri. The wounds of war have been slow to heal in this state."

"I wonder why," Torn responded dryly. "For years after the war, radical Unionists held the reins of power. Every judge and sheriff, even the governor—remember Fletcher?—was one of them. And I'm sure you recall the Union Leagues. Lynch mobs and night riders who terrorized every man, woman, and child in the state—anyone and everyone who didn't agree with their vindictive brand of politics. They were as bad as the rebel bushwhackers. Their actions served only to strengthen the resolve of die-hard secessionists."

"The radicals are out now, Clay. But the out-laws—the bushwhackers, as they're called—are still around."

"What do you want me to do?"

"One of the worst gangs has been operating just west of here, in Cass County. Thirty men, maybe more. It's hard to say with any certainty. We don't even know the identities of some of them. Farmers and store clerks by day, bandits and butchers by night. One we did know, Caleb Branson, was cap-tured in Jefferson City. At this very moment Branson is a hundred yards from here, in irons and closely guarded by three of Havelock's deputy marshals. We intend to see him tried for murder. We want the trial to take place in Cass County. And I want you to be the presiding judge."

"Why me?"

"The gang has survived this long thanks in no small part to the tolerance—and in some cases the direct assistance—of many of Cass County's citizens. These people have little liking for the banks and railroads upon which the gang preys. They look upon these bushwhackers as modern-day Robin Hoods."

"But why try Branson in Cass County? That's just begging for bloodshed."

"Several reasons. One is to prevent Branson's becoming a martyr. We want to show the people in Cass County two things. To those who sympathize with the bushwhackers, we want to demonstrate that even a man like Branson will get a fair trial. And to those who want law and order in Cass County but are too afraid of the bushwhackers to stand up for it, we want to prove that law and order will prevail. Give them a little backbone, you might say."

"I see," said Torn, noncommittal.

"It won't be easy. In fact, it will be downright dangerous. The bushwhackers may try to disrupt the trial or stop it altogether. They may try to free Branson. You never know. Their leader, Hadley Fourcade, has proved to be a . . ."

Torn's blood ran cold. His expression stopped Williams.

"What's the matter?" asked the attorney general, alarmed.

"I know all about Hadley Fourcade—but I didn't know he was leading the Cass County bushwhackers."

Williams frowned. "You know Fourcade? How?"

"We served together for a time during the war. In the same regiment. We were both born in South Carolina."

"Neighbors?" Williams looked crestfallen. "Friends, then?"

Torn's smile was bitter.

"Not friends. In fact, we've been trying to kill each other on and off for the past fifteen years."

CHAPTER 3

DECEMBER 21, 1860.

The day dawned cold and damp and dreary. A gray curtain of high clouds masked the sun's ascent. Ground-hugging mist, cotton-white, blanketed the fields on either side of the tree-lined road.

Astride a high-stepping thoroughbred, Clay Torn strove to keep his back straight and his shoulders squared beneath the cloak of dark green pilot cloth he wore against the morning chill. The temperature was well below the freezing mark, and the dampness made it worse. Bleak weather, and it was perfectly natural to hunch up and shiver. But Torn fought with fierce determination against showing any evidence of physical weakness. He was afraid it might be misconstrued by the men who rode with him down that

South Carolina road. They might think him afraid. And that would never do.

He hated to admit it even to himself, but he *was* afraid. Today, in all likelihood, he would have to kill a man, or be killed.

"There!" exclaimed Brett Yarnell, riding on Torn's left and pointing now to the right of the road. "The dueling oaks." His excitement was tainted with a sudden dose of dismay. "I see Hadley has already arrived. We're not late, are we, Cousin Stewart?"

Stewart Torn, Clay's younger brother, fished a key-winder out of his vest pocket.

"Right on time," he said.

Yarnell flashed a boyish grin. "Thank heaven for that!"

Torn resented his cousin's enthusiasm for what was about to take place. To be a minute late, of course, would imply cowardice. It was better to die than to have one's honor sullied in that way. Honor, mused Torn, was the obligation of gentlemen—and their curse. For honor's sake a man would die this day.

An errant thought—it was four days to Christmas. His twentieth Christmas. Would he live to see it? As he and his seconds turned off the road and headed for the grove, Torn cursed his lack of confidence. He was an excellent pistol shot. Everyone said so. But then, so was Hadley Fourcade.

That skill was required of every blue-blood son of the South. If nothing else he was expected to be a horseman of the highest order and a first-rate marksman. Hadley Fourcade and Clayton Torn were Clarendon County's best in both disciplines.

But Hadley held the advantage. He was a renowned duelist. He'd killed six men on the field of honor. Torn, on the other hand, had fought only one previous duel. Last year, he had challenged and killed a notorious Charleston gambler who'd insulted his sister. Even now he felt a little sick to his stomach just thinking about it.

"Brother, how do you feel?" asked Stewart.

"Fine," snapped Torn.

He realized, too late, that he should have made an effort to sound nonchalant.

Stewart forced a wan smile. Poor Stewart, thought Torn. His younger brother was a mild-mannered, even-tempered individual, amiable, sensitive, well liked by all, and the smarter of the Torn brothers. Unlike Cousin Brett—a reckless, mettlesome firebrand—Stewart always considered consequences, always looked for peaceful alternatives. He was deeply troubled now and didn't bother hiding it.

Approaching the grove—an island of century-old black oaks draped with Spanish moss and rising above a sea of mist—Torn spotted a handsome Concord buggy parked beneath the trees. A man huddled in a plaid wool blanket under the calash folding top. A hoarfrost beard and side-whiskers rendered him identifiable at a distance. Dr. Rembert.

Farther back under the sweeping limbs of the magnificent oaks were three horses. Two men stood near them. A third man sat on a massive root, leaning back against the tree trunk. Torn knew all three. The man sitting, so damnably casual, was Hadley

Fourcade. The others were Hadley's seconds, the Reklaw twins.

As they reached the edge of the grove, Stewart threw a hoping-against-hope glance over his shoulder. The hundredth such glance, calculated Torn, since their departure an hour ago from Ravenoak.

"If he did come," he told Stewart gently, "he wouldn't try to stop it."

Pale, resigned, Stewart nodded. As brothers, they needed few words to communicate. Stewart was disappointed, perhaps a little angry, at their father for not having forbidden the duel.

But Andrew Jackson Torn had adamantly refused to intervene in spite of his wife's hysterical pleas. Not that he didn't want to. He simply couldn't. He'd lived his life by the code of honor that now put his older son in peril. And to interfere would have been to destroy Clay Torn as surely as a ball fired from Hadley Fourcade's pistol.

Torn felt sorry for his father, aware of the torment he must be suffering. Andrew Torn's distress was made all the more acute by the knowledge that his own comment had provoked this deadly ritual in the first place.

Dr. Rembert climbed down out of the buggy and drew nigh with urgent strides as Torn and his seconds dismounted.

"Clayton, I urge you to put a stop to this madness. Your presence here demonstrates your courage, for which no evidence is necessary. I do not make this plea for your sake alone, but for mine and, most important, your mother's. With my own hands I delivered both you and Hadley into this world not a week apart. It grieves me to think that a moment from now I may have to pronounce one or the other of you boys dead."

"I assume you made a similar appeal to Hadley," said Torn sternly.

"Yes, yes. A futile effort I perceived it to be from the start. Hadley is apt to be a reckless fool. But you, Clayton, you have a level head on your shoulders. You must see how senseless this is."

"No, sir," Torn said stubbornly.

"These are dangerous times, boy. Emotions are at a fever pitch. Careless words are spoken in the heat of the moment. Perfectly understandable, considering the crisis we face as war looms. The South will need every one of its brave sons in the coming trial if we are to have any chance at all of success."

"I take exception to that!" cried Brett, who was too quick to take exception to anything that did not mesh with his dim understanding of affairs. "You make it sound as though we have little hope of winning independence. I beg to differ. Any one of us can whip a wagonload of those damn Yankees. They can't keep us in this infernal Union, and they won't have the guts to try, I tell you."

Amused by Brett's righteous indignation, Torn put a calming hand on his volatile cousin's shoulder. Brett Yarnell was a comfort to him in this trying situation— a strong physical presence, an uncomplicated man made of the most basic human ingredients—courage, loyalty, and simple-minded faith in his own abilities and those of his friends to succeed in every venture, no matter how risky.

"Dr. Rembert has taken an oath to save lives, Brett," said Torn. "That's all he's trying to do."

Rembert scowled. "And apparently I'm doing a dismal job of it."

"Hadley Fourcade called my father a coward and a traitor," Torn said. "He did so in my presence. I had no choice but to . . ."

Rembert made an impatient gesture.

"Absolute nonsense. Everyone knows Andrew Torn is neither. A bald-faced lie."

"A lie can travel from here to Texas before the truth can get its boots on."

Seeing that he was destined to have no luck changing Torn's mind, Rembert threw up his hands, exasperated.

"I'm wasting my time. If you two impetuous young cavaliers are so eager to throw your lives away, and over a trivial matter, then all I can do is pray for your eternal souls."

"Hadley besmirched my family's good name," snapped Torn. "That, sir, is no trivial matter."

"I shall say no more and save you the trouble of challenging an old man to a duel of honor," Rembert said with scathing asperity.

The subtle rebuke made Torn feel small. Turning away from Rembert, he doffed his hat and cloak and handed them to his brother.

"Let's get on with it," he said.

CHAPTER 4

BRETT EAGERLY UNLASHED THE PISTOL CASE from his saddle. One of the Reklaw twins, Hugh, came forward, stiffly formal, to discuss with Stewart the particulars of the forthcoming duel, as was expected of seconds.

Torn removed his frock coat, hung it on the pommel of his saddle. He had to remind himself to breathe. Down to waistcoat and cambric shirt, he keenly felt the bite of damp cold. Brett approached with the pistol case.

The matched set of caplock dueling pistols had been in the Torn family for fifty years, custom made for Clay's grandfather by the renowned Boston gunsmith Elisha H. Collier. Randall Torn had been a duelist of some repute, and Torn recalled word for word his grandfather's oft-repeated defense of the practice: "When a man knows he is going to be held accountable for his want of courtesy, he is less likely to forget his manners."

Torn's father, a peace-loving man, had managed to avoid participating in any duels. These pistols had not been fired in anger for forty years. But Torn entertained no doubts about them. They were maintained in perfect working order.

Andrew Torn's lifelong abhorrence of violence was what now brought his son to the brink of it.

It had started two days ago, when the Torns attended a levee held by the Fourcades to celebrate the state convention recently convened in Columbia for the purpose of deciding whether South Carolina would secede from the Union. No one doubted the outcome of the convention, but Andrew Torn hadn't stopped speaking up for reason and compromise. His quiet voice had been drowned out by the hue and cry for southern independence.

When Hadley applauded the convention president's opening address—read in its entirety at the levee, to a chorus of almost nonstop cheering—he had repeated the cornerstone of the speech, Danton's legendary motto of revolution: "To dare! and again to dare! and without end to dare!" Andrew Torn had wryly commented that Danton's loose tongue had ultimately bought the man a ticket to the guillotine.

Later that evening Clay had happened to overhear Hadley denouncing Andrew Torn as a traitor to his state and a coward to boot.

Torn glanced across the fog-wreathed grove at

Fourcade. Hadley was testing the weight of his own pistols, standing with Ash Reklaw. Torn had known Hadley since childhood. They had never really become friends, but neither had they ever been enemies. Until today. Hadley had a reputation as a hothead, reckless in the extreme. His comment concerning Andrew Torn had been spontaneous, his tongue loosened, perhaps, by too much to drink. But that was Hadley—talking without thinking first.

The fact that he felt no real animosity toward Hadley, considering what they were about to do, struck Torn as odd. He was sorry it had come to this. It would have been wiser to pretend he hadn't heard Hadley's remark at the levee. He could see that now. But harsh words and hasty decisions, like wasted days, could not be retrieved.

Stewart parted company with Hugh Reklaw. Torn's brother had lost all trace of color, and he relayed the agreed-upon terms to Torn with the hollow voice of a man in shock describing a hurricane or plague or some other catastrophic event.

"You and Hadley will meet, turn back to back, and at Hugh's command take ten paces. Hugh will count them off. One pistol apiece. Ash Reklaw will hold Hadley's other pistol. I suppose I must . . ."

"Brett will take my second pistol," said Torn, and gave Stewart a reassuring smile. "It isn't that I don't respect your marksmanship."

Stewart nodded, immensely relieved. It would be Brett's right and responsibility to shoot Hadley if Hadley turned and fired before taking the required ten paces. A duty, reflected Torn, that Brett Yarnell would execute with relish. Ash Reklaw would shoot Torn, should Torn not abide by the rules of fair play.

"At ten paces each man may turn and fire at will," finished Stewart. He searched Torn's face. "Clay, Dr. Rembert is right. This is sheer madness. And besides, it's against the law."

Brett laughed at that. "A law seldom enforced. At worst, Clay could be fined."

"You're assuming I'll win," said Torn.

Brett was astonished. "But of course."

"You're a student of the law, Clay," Stewart persisted, grasping at straws. "What would happen if the university learned of this?"

"I'd be expelled," replied Torn. "But I won't be talked out of it, Stewart."

After taking one of the pistols from the case, Torn loaded and capped the weapon. His hands were steady. The fear had dissipated. All that remained was a hard cold knot pressing against the base of his spine.

"Good luck, Clay," murmured Stewart.

"It's Hadley needing the luck," declared Brett.

Torn wished he could be as supremely confident as his cousin.

He walked toward Hadley, pistol held down by his side. Hadley left the Reklaw twins and moved to meet him, his stride loose and confident. Ash Reklaw stepped to one side in order to have a clear shot at Torn.

Face to face with Fourcade, Torn felt compelled to be the first to speak.

"Good morning, Hadley."

Hadley looked surprised. Was he expecting me to call it off? Torn wondered. A gesture of conciliation or loss of nerve?

"Hello, Clayton." Hadley's face was lean and dark, his mouth thin and wide, the nose long and sharply bladed. The eyes, beneath black, level brows, were a deep bottle green. He sported a thin black mustache, of which he was rather vain. His hair, black as a crow's wing, was brushed straight back from a widow's peak and gleamed with rose oil. He wore a ruffled white cambric shirt, tawny doeskin breeches tucked into riding boots. He had the look of a buccaneer, and he cultivated an image to conform with his appearance. A dark, dangerous look, a look that crept like a viper into the dreams of almost all of Clarendon County's belles.

Except, hoped Torn, Melony Hancock.

"Well, shall we get on with it?" asked Hadley, sounding bored rather than anxious. "I'd like to be home in time for breakfast."

Torn felt his face get hot. He smiled thinly. "You'll get home, Hadley. But you'll be in no condition to eat."

"Killing you, Clayton, will not interfere with my appetite."

Torn dispensed with further verbal fencing. He turned his back on Hadley, who also turned.

"Gentlemen, are you ready?" called Hugh Reklaw.

"Ready," said Torn.

"Ready," said Hadley.

"Begin. One. Two. Three . . ."

Torn was amazed at how acute his senses had

become. He could almost taste the air, could hear the crush of wet grass beneath his boots. A horse whickered, shook its head to a rattling accompaniment of bit chains.

"Four. Five. Six..."

He didn't think about dying. There was no room in his thoughts for anything or anyone but Melony. The dark-haired, green-eyed beauty who had always owned his heart—and always would. Had she risen yet this morning? Or did she still sleep not too many miles from this grove at Red Hill plantation? He had tried to keep from her the news of the duel, swearing all his friends to secrecy. Apparently he had succeeded. Had she known, she would have been here. Torn was glad she wasn't. Seeing her would have brought home to him how much he stood to lose.

"Seven. Eight. Nine..."

An icy calm overwhelmed him.

"Ten!"

He pivoted on his heel. Hadley was also turning. He seemed a long way off, but when Hadley's pistol came up, the distance closed so swiftly that it made Torn dizzy. He lifted his own arm, drew a bead. Caught his breath as white powder smoke obliterated from his view the pistol in Hadley's hand. Torn heard a soft thump. An invisible fist knocked him off-balance. No pain, just a quick sensation of a thousand pricking needles all over, followed by a breathtaking rush of numbing cold. He gazed stupidly at a spreading stain of crimson on the front of his white shirt, felt rivulets of blood down his back. The ball had struck high on the right side, an inch or two below the collarbone, and passed through.

Dragging his attention away from the wound, he looked up in time to see Fourcade hurl his empty pistol away in disgust. He stood, fists clenched, chin hiked in defiance. Torn cocked his own pistol, tried to steady his hand. He was trembling; it was difficult to hold his mark. Hadley was yelling at him, but Torn could hear only a loud buzzing in his ears. There seemed to be a great deal more fog of a sudden.

It occurred to Torn that he was losing a lot of blood and was on the verge of passing out, and that if he intended to return the favor he needed to shoot and be quick about it. The pistol was beginning to feel like a lead weight.

He squeezed the trigger, dropped his arm with a deep sigh of relief. Acrid powder smoke, smelling like rotten eggs, made his nostrils cringe and his eyes water. Blinking rapidly, he saw Hadley sprawled in the grass. The Reklaw twins were running to Fourcade's side. Torn turned away with profound regret, stepped into a bottomless pit, and began a long descent into pitch blackness. . . .

"I WISH FOR YOUR SAKE HE'D BEEN A WORSE shot," murmured George Williams when Torn had finished telling him about the duel. "And, for all our sakes, that you had been a better one."

Torn brushed a comma of dark blond hair off his forehead. "He was yelling at me when I fired. The bullet entered his mouth at an angle, tore through his cheek, cracked his jawbone, and clipped off the lobe of his left ear."

"You left your mark on him," said the attorney general. "I'm surprised he didn't try to kill you once he'd recovered."

"He did, on several occasions during the war. But at the time I thought the matter was settled. The duel had been fought."

"I come from a family of West Virginia ridge runners," Williams said. "In those parts, such a matter isn't settled until someone's six feet under."

"It wasn't like that."

"Yes, the gentleman's code of honor." Williams raised a hand to ward off Torn's reproving look. "I mean no disrespect." He rose and poured himself another brandy, then offered to refill Torn's glass. Torn declined.

"You say that you and Fourcade have been trying to kill each other off an on since the duel," said Williams. "Yet you make it sound as though the two of you bore no hard feelings toward each other at the time."

"I didn't have any hard feelings. In fact, I was relieved to learn I hadn't killed him. As for the grudge he bore me from that day on . . . well, it didn't manifest itself until later."

Williams sat down, frowning. "So you served together during the war. This puts the matter before us in a new light."

"How so?"

"Let me explain what I had in mind, and you will see. In a way, Cass County is a house divided into two factions. You have the decent law-abiding citizens on the one hand, and on the other you have those who, for a variety of reasons, like to see Fourcade's bushwhackers rule the county. And they do, Clay. For all practical purposes, they do.

"Most of the men in positions of authority in Cass County sympathize with the bushwhackers. Some because they profit from lawlessness, others because they still harbor die-hard rebel sentiments.

Through intimidation, the bushwhackers control all elections. If a man dares to run against a Fourcade-backed incumbent, his home might be burned down around his ears, or his family molested. Or he might meet with a fatal accident. Needless to say, few speak out against the bushwhackers."

"What about the army?"

"The army gave up trying to catch Fourcade and his men long ago. The bushwhackers operated with impunity during the Occupation. Confederate raiders like Forrest and Morgan and Mosby proved that a small band of men can elude a vastly superior force if they have the support of the local populace. Fourcade humiliated the army. Rode circles around it. Laughed in its face. Then we tried Pinkerton." Williams ruefully shook his head. "That was a mistake. The heavy-handed tactics of the detectives served only to turn public opinion against the government. For some time now our solution has been to ignore the problem. Hoping, I suppose, that it would go away. Letting the railroads and banks and express companies fend for themselves as best they could."

"Problems like that don't go away."

"My sentiments exactly. When Branson was apprehended, I saw a chance to strike a blow that might ultimately prove fatal to Fourcade and his raiders. Trying Branson in Cass County will show the people that one of Fourcade's men can be brought to justice, and this will provide the law-abiding citizens with hope. To carry it off I need a judge with a tremendous amount of courage. One who cannot be intimidated.

One who, first and foremost, knows how to take care of himself."

"What about the jury?"

"Yes. What about it?"

"Might not be easy finding twelve good men willing to risk their lives and their families."

"It will be difficult. You'll just have to do your best."

"I doubt we could persuade Branson to waive his right to trial by jury."

"Not to mention his counsel."

"Who will prosecute?"

"A man out of my office. John Sanford Cooke. He'll arrive in Harrisonville day after tomorrow." Williams was staring into his brandy again. "But we may have to alter our plans. You can see how your personal feud with Hadley Fourcade changes the complexion of things."

Torn had already made up his mind about that.

"I think we should go ahead."

The attorney general leaned forward, elbows planted on bony knees, and leveled a piercing gaze at Torn, as though trying to read Torn's mind.

"At the risk of offending you, I must ask: are you so willing to buy into this for the sake of law and order, or is it to fix your sights on Hadley Fourcade once more?"

Torn smiled faintly. "Would you object? He is, in the long run, the man you're after, isn't he? You want to undermine Fourcade with Branson's trial, loosen his grip on Cass County, encourage the law-abiding citizens to stand against him. We both know

Fourcade can't operate if enough of the people oppose him. Hadley knows it. It's why he resorts to fear tactics."

Williams tapped the rim of his glass with a fingernail, lips pursed. He seemed to make up his mind and gave a firm nod.

"They say you should never switch horses in midstream. I'll risk it, if you're willing to."

"Of course."

At that moment, Marshal Havelock returned. A blast of wintry air made the camphene wall lamps gutter and dance. Havelock quickly shut the door and started to remove his mackinaw coat.

"Before you get comfortable," said Torn, "I'd like to see your prisoner."

Havelock's glance at Williams was a silent query.

"If you please, Marshal." The attorney general nodded.

Torn stood. "One more question, sir. Something you may not have considered. You say Branson is charged with murder. That's all I know so far about the case you want me to try. What if the jury hears the evidence and finds him innocent? Or, if there's no jury, what if I do?"

Williams smiled, unruffled.

"Judge Torn, you have never failed to see justice done."

As they trudged through the snow side by side, Torn could tell something was bothering Havelock, and he had a hunch what that something was.

"It was a rhetorical question, Marshal," he said,

after letting the lawman stew in his own juices awhile.

Havelock's sidelong glance was sharp and suspicious. His eyes were narrowed into glittering slits against the biting wind.

"Branson shot and killed an unarmed man in the commission of a robbery, Judge. An employee of the U.S. Post Office Department. Happened in a mail car on this very railroad. There were two eyewitnesses. Branson threatened them. Laughed in their faces. They can identify him. He wasn't masked. You see, he never thought it would come to this. Swore he'd never be taken alive."

"Where are these witnesses?"

"The prosecutor will produce them."

"How is it that Branson was taken alive?"

Havelock wore a smile of grim satisfaction. "He hails from Cole County. Has a sister who lives in Jefferson City. We figured he'd stick his neck out of Cass County sooner or later to call on her. He'd done it before. We were waiting for him. Didn't give him a chance to shoot it out. I don't give people chances like that. Bad for the health. Last few weeks he's been held at Gratiot Street."

Torn nodded. Gratiot Street was the address of the prison in St. Louis. He'd put quite a few criminals behind its bars himself.

"Sounds like a pretty solid case against him."

"Damn right," Havelock said gruffly.

"I'll still have to hear his side of it."

Havelock stopped dead in his tracks.

"Branson's guilty, no question. Don't get too serious about this trial business. It's just a means to an end. The sooner you get that straight, the better off you'll be."

Torn's smile had a steely edge.

"Thanks for the advice, Marshal. It was worth every penny I paid for it."

C H A P T E R

6

A LITTLE WAY DOWN THE TRACK, LIGHTS BURNED
in the window of the Warrensburg depot. Closer
were two boxcars, coupled together on a siding. Two
men stood talking next to one of them. When Havelock spotted them, he lengthened his stride. Long
in the leg, Torn had no trouble keeping up with the
lawman.

As he drew near, Torn noticed that one of the
men wore a long sheepskin jacket and cradled a Winchester rifle in his arm. The other man wore striped
overalls and a fur-lined cap with earflaps. This man
was carrying a lantern. The boxcar's freight door
stood partially open, and a third man, armed with a
sawed-off shotgun, stood framed in the opening.

Before Torn and Havelock could reach the boxcars, the man with the lantern turned away and slogged through the snow in the direction of the depot, whistling a familiar tune.

"Who was that?" snapped Havelock, aiming this curt query at the man in the sheepskin coat. "What did he want?"

"Night watchman. Apparently the yardmaster didn't pass the word along. He just came on duty and wanted to know what we were doing here."

Havelock peered suspiciously after the railroader, now better than halfway to the depot.

"Wheeler, what did you tell him?"

"That it was federal business and to check with his superiors."

Havelock yanked furiously on his mustache, scowling. "People snooping around make me nervous. Judge, these are two of my deputies. Wheeler and Armstrong. Boys, this is Clay Torn, federal judge."

They said howdies all around. Torn's first impression of these men was favorable. They were young, confident, and probably quite capable. No bold talk or tough posturing was required. They looked him square in the eye, which he took as a good sign.

"Jennings inside?" asked Havelock.

Wheeler nodded.

"Your horse is in the next car with ours, Judge," Havelock said. "The prisoner's in here."

Armstrong gave Torn a hand up, then did Havelock the same favor.

Winter wind whistled through the slat sides of the boxcar, stirring the old straw littering the floor. The smell of cattle was pervasive. Torn guessed the car had been used to transport stock driven up the Sedalia Trail prior to its confiscation by Havelock for the task at hand. The weather being what it was, a passenger coach would have been more comfortable, but the freight car made sense, as the idea was to smuggle Branson into Cass County. Havelock wasn't taking any chances.

The third deputy, Jennings, was an older man, weathered and wiry, wearing a long black coat, puffing on a roll-your-own. Gimlet eyes beneath a hat brim pulled low flicked over Torn and then swung back to the prisoner, shackled in a corner of the car. Like Wheeler, who remained at his post outside, Jennings had a repeating rifle. Two storm lanterns illuminated the interior of the boxcar.

"There's our boy." Havelock nodded with more than a little contempt.

Torn stepped closer. Branson was huddled in a blanket, wrists and ankles shackled together. The irons were attached to lengths of stout chain, which were in turn padlocked to a heavy iron ring on a quarter-inch plate spiked to the floor.

The bushwhacker's chin was resting on his chest, and he didn't move as Torn approached, but bright ferret eyes glittered behind lank yellow hair that had fallen forward to cover his face. Branson tried to hide a weak chin with a scraggly goatee; in spite of the chin whiskers he looked boyish. His sudden smile was amiable, almost shy. Torn calculated he weighed scarcely a hundred forty pounds soaking wet, and that with a pocketful of horseshoes.

"Got the makings, friend?" asked Branson. "I could stand a smoke."

Torn shook his head.

Branson shrugged. "Well, that's okay. I'll smoke plenty when I get to hell, won't I?"

Sitting on his heels in front of the bushwhacker, Torn decided Branson was a man it would be easy to underestimate. He came across as a likable kid.

"You another tin star?" Branson asked without a trace of mockery.

"Judge," replied Torn. "Name's Torn."

"Oh. Heard about you. Yeah, now I remember. You fought for the Confederacy, just like me. Now here you are working for the damn Yankees. Shame on you, Mr. Judge."

Torn let that smooth rebuke go unchallenged. "We're taking you back to Cass County, Branson. You'll be put on trial for murder."

"You boys sure are going to a heap of trouble just to stretch my neck. Y'all could just stand me up against a wall and shoot me and we'd all have an easier go of it."

"We're not bushwhackers. We don't work that way."

"I reckon y'all got to make your killing nice and legal." Branson raised his arms, rattled the chains, and laughed as if it was all a sweet joke.

"You'll get a fair trial. I'll see to that."

Branson turned his head slightly and looked at Torn out of the corner of his eye. "You're joshing me."

"No."

"I didn't do nothing, Judge. They got the wrong man." He leaned forward, pitched his voice low, glanced at the lawmen behind Torn. "You want to know what I think? I think they're just trying to get back at me 'cause I rode with Bill Anderson's partisan rangers. Shoot, Judge, I took that damned ol' ironclad oath. War's over. 'Cept they won't let it be over. Just won't let sleeping dogs lie."

"If you're innocent, you'll go free."

"I'm innocent," pledged Branson, with perfectly crafted sincerity. "Innocent as a lamb. I'm as pure as driven snow these days."

Torn nodded, stood, and turned to face a displeased Havelock. The marshal looked as if he was about to split a seam. Inclining his head toward the door, Torn indicated they should leave. Havelock confronted him outside.

"What was all that about? How come you were coddling up to that cold-blooded killer? By God, I'm beginning to think you're the wrong man for this job, Torn. 'If you're innocent, you'll go free,' for crying out loud!"

"There are two sides to that coin, Marshal. If he's guilty, he'll hang."

"Caleb Branson's guilty as original sin, and we both know it."

"I know what I'm doing," said Torn. He changed the subject, making it clear he did not intend to discuss the matter further. "When are you going into Cass County?"

"Tomorrow. Hitch on to a westbound that pulls through here at dawn." Havelock glowered, still in high dudgeon. "We'll roll right into Harrisonville and commandeer the local lockup before anybody there knows what's happening."

Torn looked beyond Havelock at the Pullman palace car. "And the attorney general?"

"This is as far as he goes. He'll be heading east tomorrow."

"Any chance Fourcade might know your plans?"

"We've played it close to the vest."

"Just the same, I advise you to take him the rest of the way on horseback. Surely Fourcade knows by now that Branson's been captured. You've brought him all the way across Missouri by rail. Word might have leaked out. You never know." Torn thumbed over his shoulder in the direction of the depot. "That night watchman was whistling 'Dixie.'"

Havelock shook his head and started to turn away. Then he stopped, thought twice about dismissing Torn's suggestion out of hand. He looked at the lights of the Warrensburg depot and grimaced.

"We'll ride at first light."

CHAPTER 7

THEY MADE THE THIRTY MILES BETWEEN WAR-
rensburg and Harrisonville in fairly good time, considering the conditions. It was cold, but the day
dawned clear, the sky an impossible blue, the sunlight blinding on the snow. Jennings carried a block
of chewing tobacco, and the men took a chaw, then
daubed the tobacco juice under their eyes to prevent
snow blindness.

By late morning they were in Cass County. Hadley
Fourcade's domain, located on the Osage Plains, a
high tableland a hundred miles square. The plains
were scattered with rock outcroppings, and timber
stood in the countless deep draws and coulees carved
by a dozen or so tributaries of the Missouri River
and hundreds of lesser creeks. It was perfect outlaw
country. On the open high ground a man could see

for many miles and travel swiftly. If he needed to hide, a tree-choked draw was always near at hand.

The countryside was tailor-made for ambush, so they rode with rifles—in Armstrong's case, a sawed-off shotgun—laid across saddlebows. Branson was still shackled hand and foot; the chain connecting the heavy iron hames around his ankles passed beneath the barrel of his horse. Torn had to admit that Havelock had shown sense by bringing five good horses along on the trip from St. Louis, keeping the mounts in the second boxcar, available for a getaway attempt in the event the train was set upon by bushwhackers.

One deputy always ranged ahead. The others kept well apart. They steered clear of the occasional remote farm, and saw no one all day.

Late in the morning they spotted a plume of black smoke to the north, marking the progress of a train on the spur the Pacific Railroad had run to Harrisonville off the main line connecting St. Louis and Kansas City. Reaching a river a half hour later, they saw the train itself—a day coach, an express car, and several boxcars trailing a Baldwin Mogul—rattling across a trestle a hundred yards upstream.

"There goes the train we were gonna ride," remarked Havelock, with a wry glance at Torn. "Looks like they haven't had any problems so far." Studying the river, he could not refrain from making a sarcastic comment regarding how high it was running.

Torn knew the marshal was trying to nettle him, but he didn't bother defending his decision to ride to Harrisonville in a saddle rather than on iron rails. He figured foresight was worth a damn sight more than hindsight any day.

He had no evidence to indicate that Hadley knew anything about the plan to transport Branson to Harrisonville for trial. But he knew better than to underestimate Fourcade. Hadley couldn't have survived in the bandit business all these years without benefit of a superb intelligence network. He had outwitted the Pinkerton National Detective Agency and the United States Army, and his success wasn't entirely due to blind luck.

Havelock was right: the river was high, and they had to swim for it, as all agreed it would be a waste of time trying to get the horses to cross the high railroad bridge. Havelock knew of a ferry a few miles downriver, but no one, including the marshal, gave that serious consideration. If Hadley was worth his salt, every ferryman in Cass County would be a spy for the bushwhackers.

So they stripped down and swam across, wrapping their clothes in their coats and tying the bundles securely to their saddles to keep the garments as dry as possible. Branson's ankles were freed, so that he could swim alongside his horse the way the rest of them did, but his hands remained shackled together. Havelock tied one end of a rope around Caleb's neck and the other to his own saddle in case Branson got the bright idea of letting the fast-moving river carry him to freedom.

They reached the other side of the river without mishap, dried off, and dressed quickly. There was no time for a warming fire.

Pressing on, they had Harrisonville in sight as the sun plunged toward the western rim of the Osage Plains in a blaze of fire-colored glory.

"Looks peaceful enough," said Havelock, as they sat their horses on high ground and surveyed the small hamlet.

The town was nestled in the wooded embrace of a horseshoe ridge. A blue haze of woodsmoke trapped by the surrounding heights was pierced by the white steeple of a church at the northern end of what appeared to be the main street. Torn saw a number of two-story brick and stone buildings lining the street. A creek skirted the town, and beside the creek stood a gristmill. Near the mill were the train depot, railyard, and turnplate; the spur terminated at Harrisonville.

"We better wait for night before going in," advised Torn.

Havelock groaned. What little warmth the sun had provided was already a fond memory, and none of them were partial to the idea of staying out in this weather any longer than necessary. But only the marshal was inclined to take issue with Torn.

"You're as cautious as a small dog with a big bone, Judge. The train got in all right. I reckon we will, too."

"Just a suggestion, Marshal. Take it or leave it."

Tugging ferociously on his mustache, Havelock looked at the town, at Torn, back at the town. "You put a lot of stock in this Fourcade feller."

"I've seen him work."

Torn wasn't willing to argue the point. Instead,

he waited impassively for Havelock to make up his mind, leaving it to the marshal to call the shots here. Havelock seemed capable enough, but a wall of animosity stood between them. Torn didn't know why, or what the animosity stemmed from, but it was there. He could sense it, and he wanted to know— had to know—if Havelock was going to let it color his judgment. If he did, then they all had a big problem.

"Okay." Havelock sighed, disgruntled. "We'll hole up."

"Down in that draw," suggested Torn. He kicked the dun gelding into motion to lead the way down a steep shoulder into the blue shadows of the wooded depression. The snow, firm and crusty on the high ground, was stirrup-high powder under the trees, and the horses labored.

Runoff had built a deadfall around a hickory tree that had fallen into a jumble of gray granite boulders. On the downhill side of this natural barricade they found shelter among the rocks. Here they settled in to wait for nightfall. None of the lawmen even suggested a fire for warmth. Torn was happy to know he had professionals backing him. A fire was too risky. For all they knew, the area was swarming with bushwhackers. Better safe than sorry.

Encouraged by the manner in which these men conducted themselves, Torn proceeded to explain what he had in mind for their night call on Harrisonville.

CHAPTER 8

TORN'S PLAN WENT LIKE CLOCKWORK—AT FIRST.

Havelock knew where the jail was located—in one of those two-story stone buildings on the main street. They left their horses in the rocky ravine, near the creek that danced down off the horseshoe ridge, and proceeded on foot with the utmost stealth, carrying their long guns. The bone-biting cold had driven everyone else indoors. The only living thing Torn saw was a stray dog skulking away with tail tucked.

They paused a moment in the black-as-pitch shadows of an alley alongside the jail.

"Well, Judge, no welcoming committee" was Havelock's sardonic observation.

"Right," said Torn. "Just a nice quiet little town."

"Yep. Farming community. One saloon, and it's in the hotel. They call it a barroom. Harrisonville isn't like those gallop-and-gunshot towns on the cattle trails. Jail's plenty big, I guess because this is the county seat. The sheriff's office and private quarters downstairs, cellblock upstairs."

Torn glanced at Branson. As a precaution, the bushwhacker had been gagged. It was beginning to look to Torn as though all his precautions had been for naught.

"Let's get inside, for chrissake," groused Havelock, clearly fed up with Torn's prudent approach. "It's cold enough out here to freeze the horns off a steer."

"You and I will go first," said Torn. "Jennings, you watch our back trail. Wheeler, you cover the street from the end of the alley. Branson is your responsibility, Armstrong."

With a curt nod, Armstrong planted his scattergun against Branson's chest, pinning the bushwhacker to the wall.

"Good God," muttered Havelock, exasperated. "Listen, Judge . . ."

"Come on, Marshal."

Torn led the way, treading softly on the warped planks of the boardwalk in front of the jailhouse. Havelock followed, his spurs singing against the wood. Shaking his head, Torn realized the marshal was too stubborn to lighten his step.

Reaching the door, Torn put his back to the wall and slowly scanned the street, a wide and empty expanse of snow and frozen mud, crisscrossed with the tracks of wagons and the hoofprints of horses. Now, though, there wasn't a horse or wagon or living soul in sight. Most of the windows were dark. Very faintly, he heard a baby's squall. Was it too quiet? Or was Harrisonville just a tranquil town where the sidewalks were rolled up at sundown?

Havelock made to go right on in, but the door was locked, and the marshal grunted in surprise as he fetched up against heavy wooden beams reinforced with strap iron. He glanced at Torn, who nodded, Winchester .44–40 held ready. Havelock pounded on the door with his fist.

"Who is it?" came a voice from within.

"Frank Havelock, United States marshal. Open up."

A bolt was thrown. The door creaked open. A paunchy, narrow-shouldered man stood in the doorway. His features were too small for his big, round, heavy-jowled face, and they were pinched too close together. Nervous, squinty eyes flicked back and forth, back and forth, between Torn and Havelock, never settling for long on either man.

"You the sheriff?" Havelock saw the ball-pointed star pinned to the man's blanket coat, but asked anyway.

"Yeah. Name's Spivey. You say you're a U.S. marshal? How do I know that to be true?"

With a thin, barely tolerant smile, Havelock yanked his mackinaw coat open to display the badge, a small star set in a circlet of steel.

"What can I do for you, Marshal?"

Torn peered past Spivey into the dark interior of the jail. "Were you sleeping, Sheriff?"

"Huh? Oh, yeah. Just about to turn in."

Torn gave him a skeptical once-over. The man was fully clothed and had a gun strapped to his hip.

"I'm borrowing your jail, Sheriff," Havelock announced. "We've got a federal pri—"

"Just a minute," Torn interrupted, and started through the door.

Spivey backstepped—it was obvious that Torn was coming in whether he got out of the way or not. Torn saw the dim outlines of a desk and stove in the front room. A fire had burned down to orange embers in the stove, giving off a trifle of light. Not nearly enough to suit Torn. The window shutters were closed and barred. A door to the back room was also closed. A steep staircase to his left led to the cellblock on the second floor.

"Anybody up there?" Torn asked Spivey.

"Huh? Uh, no. Cells are empty. Usually are. This is a nice quiet—"

"So I've heard."

"Seldom have any problems."

You do now, thought Torn. He said, "In Cass County? That surprises me."

"What's this about borrowing my jail?" asked Spivey.

"Temporary," said Havelock. "I've got a—"

"How about some light in here?" Torn suggested.

"Christ!" rasped Havelock, aggravated. "You going to let me finish a sentence or not?"

Spivey turned to the desk. Heading for the door to the back room, Torn heard a lamp chimney rattle, the scrape and hiss of a match, the faint scent of sulfur followed by the stench of kerosene burning.

Amber light threw his exaggerated shadow against the wall in front of him.

"Where are you going?" asked Spivey.

"Just having a look around," Torn replied pleasantly.

Havelock spun on his heel, strode to the door, and stepped across the threshold.

"Wheeler! You and the others get in here."

Torn was reaching for the doorknob when he heard a telltale squeak directly overhead. Weight being put on a loose floorboard. He looked up sharply, a reflex, then fired a suspicious glance at Spivey. The sheriff was looking at the staircase.

Torn snapped off a warning. "Havelock! It's a trap!"

Boots pounded on the stairs—two men descending in a big hurry. Cursing, Havelock whirled. Torn spun around, swept the lamp off the desk with the barrel of his Winchester, whirled as the door to the back room burst open and a man stepped out, gun blazing.

CHAPTER 9

TORN DIVED FOR THE NEAREST COVER. HE HIT the top of the desk, skidded across, and fell none too gracefully off the other side. His long legs struck the chair, knocking it over. Bullets slapped into the desk, splintering wood. Several more guns spoke, filling the office with deafening gun thunder, shredding the darkness with quick stabs of six-shooter lightning.

Caught in the crossfire, Spivey yelped like a kicked dog. Torn heard a thump—a body falling. Leaving the Winchester on the floor, he drew his Colt .45 Peacemaker. The pistol was the more suitable weapon for close-quarter killing.

He hiked himself around the desk on his elbows, saw muzzle-flash across the room, where the staircase was located. Hot lead seared the air, peppered the walls. Where was Havelock? Torn didn't want to shoot the marshal by mistake. His question was answered by the sharp crack of a long rifle being fired—a sound quite different from the throaty boom of short-barreled pistols. Had to be Havelock. The shot came from outside, on the boardwalk. The marshal was firing through the open front door.

Satisfied, Torn fired three rounds across the room, ducked as a hail of bullets replied. Twice more he fired, reaching up and over the desk, shooting blind. Couldn't see much, anyway. He heard the crack of timber, the heavy thud of another body striking the floor. This was followed by the pounding of boots on the stairs, someone running up to the cellblock. The level of gunfire was significantly reduced. One bullet left in the Colt, thought Torn, and no guarantee I'll have the time to reload. A pistol barked from the door to the back room.

Havelock stopped shooting. So did the man in the back room doorway. Footsteps beat a tattoo on the boardwalk. Havelock barked, "Cover the back!" Torn strained to hear any sound that might sort out the confusion inherent in night fighting. He couldn't see much of anything. With the windows shuttered— even a thread of moonlight would have helped—the jailhouse was as black as the ace of spades.

Torn groped for the Winchester, put his hand in something wet. Kerosene. Spilled out of the brass base of the lamp he had knocked over. He felt around, cut his finger on a shard of glass from the broken chimney. He found the base and by touch confirmed that the wick was still in place.

A shot shattered the silence. The man in the back room doorway, Torn surmised. No hogleg accompaniment from the staircase. What had happened to the two ambushers there? Torn assumed one was down and the other had retreated upstairs, then reminded himself that assumptions could get a man killed.

Some light had to be shed on the subject, and he had a good idea how to do just that. He searched his pockets, found his match case, and lit the lamp wick with a strike-anywhere. Huddled behind the bullet-riddled desk, he lobbed the lamp base across the room. It struck the wall near the staircase and hit the floor with a clatter, spewing kerosene. Tongues of flame licked the wall, rushed across the floor. The man at the door to the back room fired instinctively at the sound of the falling lamp. Torn rose from behind the desk and fired. His last bullet punched the man square in the chest and dropped him.

Torn drew a deep breath and looked around the office. One of the men he'd glimpsed charging down the staircase now lay on the floor, sprawled in the wreckage of the banister he had crashed through. Spivey lay on his face in the middle of the room, his head resting in a pool of blood. Torn reckoned the sheriff had been hit by a stray bullet fired by one of the ambushers.

Spivey had been part and parcel of the ambush. Of this Torn had no doubt. Attorney General Williams had warned that most of Cass County's elected officials were in Hadley's hip pocket. Apparently, such had been the case with Spivey, who had learned, the hard way, a truth about bushwhackers: they didn't give a tinker's damn for anyone caught in the middle.

Havelock stormed through the door. His rifle swung in Torn's direction, and Torn had a bad moment, wondering if he was going to be the second man shot dead, accidental-like, tonight. But the marshal recognized Torn and eased the hammer down. He gave the three dead men a cursory glance, then turned his attention to the fire.

"Give me a hand, Judge, before this place goes up in smoke."

"Careful," cautioned Torn. "One left. Upstairs."

The sound of glass shattering from the second-story verified this, followed by a shout from out back, then two gunshots. Havelock was halfway up the stairs when Wheeler entered through the front door and said, "Jennings nailed one coming out an upstairs window."

"Put that fire out," said Havelock. "I'll have a look-see up there."

Torn shrugged out of his greatcoat and used the garment to smother the blue flames on the floor. He hated to ruin a perfectly good coat; he had to feed and clothe himself and pay all his other expenses on a salary of two dollars a day. But he'd started the fire, and so he felt responsible for putting it out. There was no time to call the local volunteer fire brigade, assuming Harrisonville had one. The walls of native stone were not at risk, but the fire could quickly gut the interior of the building, consuming floors and ceiling and roof, and could conceivably spread to other structures on the main street. All it took was a couple of burning embers carried on the wind. Torn didn't want to see the town go up in smoke.

Wheeler grabbed a coffeepot off the stove and doused the burning kerosene on the wall with its cold black contents. Dense smoke swirled on a cold draft of winter air gusting through the open front door.

With the fire extinguished, the office was again plunged into darkness. Wheeler found another lamp in the back room, lighted it, and brought it into the office as Havelock descended the stairs, rifle shoulder-racked.

"All clear." He looked at Torn with grudging respect. "You made short work of them, Judge."

"Your deputy got one. And I think the sheriff here was hit by one of the bushwhackers."

"Wheeler, fetch the others." Havelock slumped heavily on the corner of the desk. His face was etched with pain, his complexion ashen gray. Torn saw the bullet hole in the mackinaw coat. The marshal held his left arm rigid. Rivulets of scarlet blood snaked from under the sleeve of the coat onto his hand, dripped from his fingers.

"How bad?" asked Torn.

"Just nicked."

Torn lifted the mackinaw. Havelock's shirt was soaked with blood. He'd been hit in the shoulder.

"Should be a doctor in town," said Torn.

"No. A Cass County doctor might let his knife slip. Depends on where his loyalty lies, and around here you can never tell."

"The bullet's still in you, Marshal. It's got to come

out, and the wound needs to be cleaned."

"Jennings can do it. He's dug lead out of me before."

Torn reached under his frock coat and pulled out his saber-knife.

"Lord," breathed Havelock. "Never seen a neck blister like that before."

It was no ordinary knife by any means. The blade was fifteen inches long, almost two inches wide. The hilt sported a brass single-guard bow. Torn carried the weapon in a sheath strapped upside down against his rib cage, secured by a custom-made shoulder harness.

The saber-knife was his ace in the hole. Having it concealed in this way had saved his bacon on more than one occasion. It had once belonged to a sergeant of the guard at Point Lookout, the prisoner-of-war camp where Torn and thousands of other Confederate captives had been incarcerated. During his escape from that hellhole, Torn had killed the sadistic sergeant with his own saber. The blade had later broken. Torn had honed it down to its present length.

"I can dig that slug out of you, Marshal," he said.

Havelock's eyes were cold and black as the grave, and just as friendly. There it was again, thought Torn—that deep animosity.

"We're on the same side," he said crisply. "I won't let it slip, if that's what you're worried about."

"Jennings will see to that," said Havelock, obstinate. "I trust him. I'm not sure about you just yet, Judge."

Torn nodded. At least the man was honest.

"Fine," he said, sheathing the saber-knife. "But if we don't start working together, Marshal, we might get buried together."

CHAPTER 10

THE DEPUTIES CAME IN WITH BRANSON. HAVE-lock told Armstrong to lock the prisoner in a cell and stand guard over him.

"A man jumped out an upstairs window," Jennings reported laconically. "I plugged him. Dragged his carcass around to the front. Looks like you took some lead yourself, Frank."

"Dig it out of me, Les. Wheeler, make yourself useful and drag these three out and put them with the rest of the garbage."

As Jennings took a gander at Havelock's gunshot wound, Wheeler went to work dragging the corpses out by the heels. Coming back from his second trip, he remarked, "Some folks gathering out there."

Torn stepped out to have a look. A dozen or so men stood across the street in front of a darkened general store. Some carried lanterns. Some were armed. All looked as if they'd dressed in haste. More men, singly and in pairs, were coming from both ends of the street. Wheeler dragged another body out of the jailhouse, left it alongside the other two, and walked over to stand shoulder to shoulder with Torn.

"Reckon we'll have more trouble tonight?" asked the deputy, as casually as if he were asking Torn if he thought it might snow before morning.

"I'll go find out. Cover me."

Torn started across the street.

A man left the group and came forward to meet him—a tall, lantern-jawed man with a shock of white hair, who walked with a decided limp. He wore an overcoat, and Torn couldn't tell if he was armed.

"What's going on here?" asked the man, face to face with Torn, his tone imperious. "What's the meaning of this, sir? Who are you?"

Despite the man's bluster, Torn could tell he was scared right down to his socks.

"Clay Torn, federal judge. That man behind me is a deputy United States marshal. Who are you?"

Torn was quiet, courteous. His attitude seemed to reassure the man, who exhaled sharply and relaxed.

"Josiah Armbruster, sir. The mayor of Harrisonville. What in heaven's name happened here, Judge?"

"It's a long story."

"Shots have been fired in my town. Men killed. I demand to know . . ."

Torn held up a hand. "Three of Hadley Fourcade's men were waiting in the jail to ambush us. Your sheriff was their accomplice."

"Bill Spivey? What are you saying?"

"I already said it. Hadley's men are dead. And you're going to need a new sheriff."

Armbruster was aghast. "You killed Bill Spivey?"

"One of the bushwhackers gunned him down. He was in the way. I'm sure you've lived around here long enough, Mayor, to know how they operate."

Distraught, Armbruster pressed a hand against his forehead as though trying to tell if he was running a fever. Torn was convinced that Armbruster hadn't known about the ambush in advance. The news came as a complete surprise to him.

"I don't understand," muttered the Harrisonville mayor. "Why did this happen?"

"Like I said, a long story. I only want to tell it once. Call a town meeting for tomorrow. What I've got to say, the whole town needs to hear."

Armbruster looked scared all over again. "You say they were Fourcade's men?"

"Right. Tell your constituents back there that I've come here to put an end to Hadley Fourcade and his gang once and for all. The name's Torn. Clay Torn."

"Yes, yes. You told me."

"Just wanted to make sure you got it right, Mayor. You see, I figure Hadley will hear about this quicker than a hair trigger. And I want to make sure he knows I'm after him."

Armbruster stared at Torn as he would at a madman.

"God help you, sir," he whispered fervently. "God help us all."

Torn smiled thinly. "God helps those who help themselves."

He turned away.

"What . . . what about those bodies, Judge Torn?"

"Be best if you kept your people away from the jail tonight," replied Torn. "Worry about the living, Mayor, not the dead. It's right cold. The dead will keep till morning."

A bottle of Old Crow was found in the sheriff's desk, and by the time Jennings had finished cutting the bullet out of Havelock and cauterizing the wound, the marshal had polished off every last drop of whiskey. He stayed conscious during the operation and acquitted himself well, but shortly thereafter stretched out on the desk, heaved a deep sigh, and quietly passed out.

Torn took Wheeler along to retrieve their horses from the ravine at the edge of town. They found a livery stable fifty yards north of the jail on the main street. The crowd had dispersed; the street once more was quiet. The livery was closed up, unattended. Most of the stalls were empty. They unsaddled the horses, rubbed them down, fed and watered them.

"Someone should stay here, make sure our horses don't turn up missing," said Torn.

Wheeler grinned. "I'll take orders from you, Judge. No need to step lightly."

"Fine. Get up in the loft, then. You can watch the street from there at the same time."

"Suits me. I'll find a nice warm pile of hay."

"Keep your eyes open. I have a feeling Fourcade is close by."

"Sounds like you know this Fourcade feller."

"We were in the war together."

"The war." Wheeler's easy grin vanished. "My pa went off to fight in that war. Never came back. They said he just disappeared at the Battle of Chickamauga."

"Sorry to hear that," said Torn. It happened that way all too often. So many thousands slain that it was impossible to identify all the casualties. Missing, presumed dead. Their remains left to rot on blood-soaked battlegrounds. And loved ones left to wonder . . .

"It's the worst thing of all," he added, soft-spoken. "Not knowing."

Wheeler watched him put his hand over his heart and thought it a curious gesture. He did not know about the photograph of Melony Hancock that Torn carried in the inside pocket of his black frock coat. He was unaware that Torn was thinking at that moment of the woman he loved, the woman he had searched for all these years since the war, all the while not knowing if she was alive or dead.

"I wanted to fight," said Wheeler pensively. "But I was too young."

"We'll have a war here before we're done."

"What do you think Fourcade will do, Judge?"

"What you least expect. He'll hit hard and fast, and at just the right moment."

"You sound sure about him."

"I am. He and I learned how to wage war from a master."

"Who was that?"

"General J. E. B. Stuart."

CHAPTER 11

JUNE 12, 1862.

"We must be going to join Stonewall in the Valley."

Torn did not respond to his brother's conjecture. He and Stewart rode stirrup to stirrup at the head of a column of cavalry trotting down a dusty Virginia road. It was pitch dark; they'd broken camp at Kilby's Station shortly after two in the morning, and Torn calculated they'd been on the march for more than two hours.

He looked east. In another hour or so the sky would begin to pearl with dawn light. McClellan and his formidable Army of the Potomac lay in that direction. A massive federal invasion force, well led, well trained, and well equipped. Torn was sensitive to the menacing presence of this impressive war machine that had in the past several months inched its way inexorably closer to Richmond, up the peninsula between the James and York rivers.

"So what do you think, Clay?" pressed Stewart. "Where are we going? Why won't they let us know?"

"When General Stuart wants to tell us, we'll know," replied Torn.

Turning in his saddle, he looked back at what little he could see of the column-by-fours trailing behind in a pale haze of summer dust visible even at night. The men directly behind him were the squadron of volunteer cavalry, which he captained. The only contingent of South Carolina troops in a force of twelve hundred men—all cavalry, with a section of horse artillery ably commanded by Lieutenant James Breathed. Most of the other units were Virginian. Stuart had asked for the best squadron in the Hampton Legion. Wade Hampton—the man who had raised and equipped the legion, a combined unit of the best South Carolina infantry, cavalry, and artillery—had selected Torn's squadron for the honor.

The troopers rode under strict orders to keep quiet. Only an occasional cough punctuated the creak of saddle leather, the rattle of bridle chains and sabers, the whicker of horses. The squadron formed the vanguard of Stuart's column, and everyone was prepared for a clash with an enemy patrol before the day was done.

Torn and his men knew this Virginia countryside as well as any son of the Old Dominion. They'd distinguished themselves in more than a dozen engagements since the previous March, when McClellan's army had floated down the Potomac and embarked on a flank attack against Richmond.

Personally, Torn hoped they were not bound for the Shenandoah to join Stonewall Jackson's small army. Jackson's Valley Campaign had been successful to the extent that it tied up vastly superior federal forces that would otherwise have reinforced McClellan. Little Mac already outnumbered the beleaguered Confederates dug into defensive positions on the outskirts of Richmond. But in Torn's opinion, Jackson's campaign was a sideshow. The big battle— the conflict upon which hinged the future of the Confederacy—would be fought here, on the peninsula, and Torn did not want to miss it.

Tonight, though, they were heading north, on the road to Louisa Court House, and with some dismay Torn realized that every mile put behind them took them that much farther away from the two great armies confronting each other within hearing of Richmond's church bells.

A lone horseman emerged from the gloom, coming toward them. It was William Farley, the scout. Torn was glad to see him. Farley hailed from South Carolina. He and Torn had attended the University of Virginia together. A man of modest bearing and a lust for adventure, Farley was much relied upon by Stuart, entrusted with the most perilous missions. He was daring, dauntless, and extremely intelligent. Torn assumed that, as always, Farley carried a book of Shakespeare in the pocket of his plain brown coat.

The scout always tried to keep the best available horse under his saddle, and Torn admired the handsome lines of the bay hunter Farley rode tonight.

The mount had been hard run and was lathered from stem to stern.

"Good to see you, Bill," said Torn. "They told me you were up ahead looking for trouble. Find any?"

Farley flashed his trademark quick grin. He was a slender young man with mahogany-brown hair, laughing eyes, and a soft voice, a favorite with the ladies. He swung the bay hunter around to fall in alongside the Torn brothers.

"I watered this nag in the South Anna River and saw nary a blue coat to shoot at."

Torn heard a grumble from behind him and looked around to identify Brett Yarnell, the squadron's standard-bearer, as the source of this discontented sound.

"You have something to say, Corporal?" asked Torn.

"Since you asked, Captain," replied Yarnell testily. "I'm wondering, since I joined this army to fight damn Yankees, why I'm going where they *aren't*, rather than where they are."

Torn repressed a smile. The bars on his short gray tunic weighed heavy on his shoulders at such moments, when, as a commanding officer, he was required to treat his men like soldiers rather than friends or, in Brett's case, relatives.

"I venture to say it's because you have orders to do so," he answered coolly.

Yarnell was stung by Torn's strict tone, and the night wasn't dark enough to conceal his tight-lipped scowl.

A horseman arrived from farther back along the

column, and Torn found himself scowling at Hadley Fourcade.

"So it's you, Farley," said Fourcade. "What news?"

"Morning, Lieutenant." Farley was cordial, but his tone of voice lacked the affection evident during his earlier exchange with Torn. "Just saying hello. I must ride back and find the general. With your permission, gentlemen."

He swept an old flop-brimmed farmer's hat off his head with a cavalier flourish and kicked the bay hunter into a forward lunge, wheeled the horse around, and galloped south past the squadron. Torn believed Farley would find Stuart and his staff at the head of the main column, a quarter mile or so behind the South Carolina vanguard.

"Did Farley see anything up the road?" asked Fourcade.

Torn bit down on a sharp retort. Fourcade was one of his lieutenants—Stewart was the other. The disrespect in Hadley's tone was obvious. One might have thought him the commanding officer, requesting a report from a subordinate. Like all units in the Confederate army, the squadron elected its own officers. Hadley had campaigned hard for the captaincy, but Torn had won the job hands down. He had demonstrated, time and time again since then, that the men had made the right choice, and that fact did not improve Hadley's disposition.

"No sign of federals," Torn said curtly, begrudging him even this information. Hadley's desire to know what lay ahead was not in itself untoward. "Now I'll thank you to return to your troops, Lieutenant."

He could feel the heat of Hadley's anger. Torn had intended to provoke Fourcade with the curt dismissal. There was bad blood between them—had been since the duel a year and a half ago—and he accepted this as a fact of life.

Hadley stroked the scar on his cheek—the scar Torn had given him. Then he wheeled his horse around and rode away.

"I don't envy you," Stewart said glumly.

"What do you mean?" asked Torn.

"It's just that, for most of us, the enemy is always in our front. But your most dangerous enemy, brother, is at your back."

They made twenty-two miles that day. Their route took them by Emmanuel Church, over Brook Run, past Yellow Tavern, across the tracks of the Richmond, Fredericksburg and Potomac Railroad. They passed numerous farms. The people came to the roadside to greet them, offering fruit, biscuits, cups of water. The old men saluted and wished they were younger, the women waved handkerchiefs and aprons, the girls flirted, and worshipful boys ran alongside.

Soon after dark the order came to stop for the night. They bivouacked on Winston Farm, near the town of Taylorsville, close to the South Anna, which merged with the Pamunkey River less than ten miles to the east. Everyone knew that farther down the Pamunkey stood a village called White House, and spies had reported that White House was the site of a major federal supply depot. The Pamunkey itself was diligently patrolled by Union gunboats.

No campfires were allowed. Yesterday the men had cooked three days' worth of rations. Torn had heard the prevailing gossip: they were going on a foray against McClellan's right flank. He prayed that this was more than just wishful thinking.

Tomorrow would tell.

CHAPTER

12

JUNE 13, 1862.

Torn slept soundly, having taught himself to do so
on the eve of battle.

Rocket signals roused the camp in the murky gray
of a fog-wreathed dawn. No bugles blew noisy rev-
eille. Men and horses were quickly fed. The column
got under way. Within the hour, Torn was ordered
to turn the vanguard east on the road to Hanover
Court House. He and the twelve hundred men strung
out behind him were vastly relieved.

Later that morning all field officers were sum-
moned to council. Torn left his brother in command
of the ongoing squadron and rode back to the meeting. Field and staff officers, still mounted, were gathered near a split-rail fence just off the road.

Stuart presided, and every eye was fixed on him.

Though he was only five-ten in height, his robust build—broad shoulders, massive chest, and brawny arms—gave him an appearance of great physical strength. As usual, his face was florid, his ice blue eyes piercing.

His uniform was the most outlandish in the army—not even George Pickett could outdo him in this regard. A black plume adorned his wide-brimmed brown hat. A short gray cavalry tunic was covered with braid and rows of bright buttons. A scarlet-lined cape was draped over his shoulders; a yellow sash encircled his waist. Golden spurs were strapped to high jackboots. A pistol and a French saber were his weapons. The press called him the Murat of the Confederacy.

"Gentlemen," he said, the voice that could ring clear as a bell over the din of battle now muted to barely more than a whisper, "we are embarking on a scout movement behind the enemy. We will circle his flank, gather intelligence on the strength and position of those of his units north of the Chickahominy, and destroy those of his supplies and lines of communication as we can without engaging in a pitched battle. General Lee has cautioned me not to unnecessarily hazard this command. So I urge all of you to exercise prudence and vigilance."

He looked about him, at first very serious in expression. Then Torn saw the thick cinnamon-colored beard move, and the sweeping mustache curl upward. Stuart's white teeth flashed in a grin, and a mischievous fire glimmered in those glacial eyes.

"Prudence and vigilance aside," he added wryly,

"I believe it is possible for us to ride completely around McClellan."

A murmur of surprise and excitement greeted this announcement. Torn smiled with cold satisfaction. That was just the kind of daredevil show that would shake the confidence of the federals and raise the morale of the Confederate army. Stuart noted Torn's reaction and gave a short, approving nod.

"Some might call this madness," said Stuart, chuckling. "But let me assure you, there is method to it. That's all, gentlemen. God bless the Confederacy."

Torn and the other officers returned to their commands.

The column continued east, through woodlands, past fields of young corn. The day was clear, the summer morning soon hot and dusty. Well before noon Farley reappeared.

"Bluebirds ahead, at Hanover Court House," the scout informed Torn. "I asked around, but nobody can say for sure how many. They showed up early this morning. Probably just a patrol."

Torn sent Farley back in the direction of town to see what he could see, and dispatched a trooper to deliver the news to Stuart. He ordered the squadron on, sent out flankers. The trooper returned with a message from Stuart.

"Fitz Lee and the First Virginia will swing around in an attempt to cut off the enemy. We're to give them a quarter hour to get in position, and then we'll attack."

Torn nodded, halted the squadron, sent word back

down the line for the men to see to their weapons. While the squadron sat their horses in the road, he consulted his watch. Tried not to consult it too often. The fifteen minutes dragged, seeming like an hour. His pulse had quickened, and his mouth was dry. Action was imminent, and by now these symptoms were familiar to him. Part of it was fear. He wasn't foolish enough to deny this to himself, though pride prevented him from admitting it to others. He'd survived dozens of engagements, been witness to the horrors of war, and these days a degree of fatalism tempered the fear of dying, diminished it.

Before the fifteen minutes had passed, shots rang out up-road. Torn didn't hesitate; he led the squadron toward the town at the charge.

They found nothing but the dust of the enemy. The squadron's prey, somehow forewarned, had been flushed. Torn pressed on in pursuit, but caught not a glimpse of the bluecoats. He met Fitz Lee's embarrassed Virginians, who'd blundered into a marsh and failed to reach the road in time to cut off the federals' hasty retreat.

Torn took his men back to Hanover Court House, swallowing his disappointment. The rest of the column had by now arrived, and the men were milling in the streets. Torn saw Stuart on the steps of the quaint brick courthouse where Patrick Henry had made many of his most stirring speeches. The general was questioning a handful of townsfolk. One of his staff officers searched Torn out.

"The general wishes you to press on with all haste toward Old Church, Captain, and asks that you engage the enemy at the first opportunity."

It was no sooner said than done. The rapid march took its toll as the blazing summer sun climbed the sky, and heat shimmered out of the cornfields. The squadron trotted past Taliaferro's Mill and Hawes Shop, the wagon factory and forge. Farley, the scout, ranged ahead. Torn tirelessly scanned the terrain south and east. He was sure the Yankees weren't far away. Military logic indicated they would stand and fight for Old Church. The town stood at a vital crossroad. Supply trains crossing the Pamunkey on two nearby ferries had to pass through Old Church to reach McClellan's right wing.

A mile from the village Farley appeared with word that this was so. Two squadrons of the Fifth U.S. Cavalry were formed across the road not far ahead.

Hadley rode up. "I'm tired of eating your brother's dust," he told Torn, with a hostile glance at Stewart. "I insist you let my men lead the attack."

"Get back where you belong, Lieutenant," snapped Torn.

Infuriated, Hadley clenched rein leather so tightly that his horse balked and pranced. He swung his glower from Torn to Stewart. "You bear in mind that the date of my commission in the legion gives me command of the squadron when your brother falls."

"You mean if he falls," said Stewart coldly.

Hadley savagely got his mount under control and left them.

"He'll kill you if he gets the chance, Clay," warned Stewart.

Torn shook his head. The federals lay in wait,

ready to give battle. He had no time to worry about Hadley Fourcade. Standing in his stirrups, he drew his saber, held it overhead, and turned to his troops.

"Draw sabers! Charge!"

The squadron swept forward, sun flashing on steel. . . .

CHAPTER 13

TORN LEFT WHEELER IN THE LIVERY STABLE AND quartered across the dark, quiet street to the Harrisonville jail. He gave the street a careful study. Upon reaching the jail, he had the layout clearly etched in his mind—every building in relation to others, every doorway, every window, every alley. He studied it as he had many battlegrounds during the war.

Jennings had barred the door, so he had to identify himself to get inside. Marshal Havelock was still out cold. Torn went upstairs to the cellblock—four strap-iron cells in a row, a wide corridor separating them from the stairwell. Each cell had a single small window, four panes of glass with thick iron rods securely set into the stone of the foot-thick walls.

In one of the cells, Branson was sprawled on a

narrow bunk, whistling "Bonnie Blue Flag," one of the Confederacy's favorite tunes. The deputy, Armstrong, was tilted against a wall at the end of the corridor next to a wood-burning stove, the scattergun cradled in his arms. His was a good position; he could watch the stairs and all the windows as well as the prisoner.

"Everything all right?" asked Torn.

Armstrong nodded.

At the other end of the corridor was the window the bushwhacker had gone through. It didn't have bars, and now it didn't have much in the way of glass, either. A bitter cold wind whistled past the jagged glass teeth still anchored in the frame.

"I'll get some wood for that stove," said Torn, "and something to cover this window."

"I'd be obliged."

Torn went back downstairs.

"The cellblock windows don't have shutters," he informed Jennings. "We'll need to do something about that tomorrow."

"Sounds like we're fixin' to fort up."

Torn nodded. "Clear shots into the cellblock from a number of rooftops around here. And Hadley knows, I'm sure, how to make bombs. Smoke or fire."

The deputy was cutting a corner off his block of tobacco with a clasp knife, his creased brown features impassive.

"How many men you reckon ride with Fourcade?"

"I was told twenty or thirty."

"We're a mite outgunned," said Jennings, a calm

observation devoid of apprehension. "Think any of the folks hereabouts have the grit to fight outlaws?"

"To some of these people, Fourcade and his men are heroes, not outlaws. Our job is to prove to the rest that the law can win against the bushwhackers. Otherwise they won't risk standing against Fourcade's gang."

The deputy looked around, chewing reflectively, noting the bloodstains, the fire-scorched wall and floor, the unconscious Havelock.

"They knew we were coming, didn't they?"

Torn nodded. He hadn't been surprised by the ambush. He recalled the night watchman at the Warrensburg rail yard, whistling "Dixie." That man might have been a spy for Fourcade. Or it might have been someone else, somewhere along the line, who'd found out about the clandestine rail transfer of Caleb Branson from St. Louis to Cass County.

Hadley's tactics had been sound. He hadn't hit the train supposedly transporting Branson, knowing that this was what his enemy—the law—expected him to do. Instead, he'd waited for the marshal to deliver his prisoner to Harrisonville, using Spivey to set the trap, banking on the element of surprise. He'd been betting that Havelock and his deputies might lower their guard upon arriving without mishap at their destination.

His one mistake had been sending too few bushwhackers to get the job done. Torn wondered if Hadley had become overconfident. He'd had the run of Cass County for quite some time now, with little or no opposition.

"That Cooke feller, the prosecutor, is supposed to get here tomorrow, isn't he?" asked Jennings.

"Right. And he's bringing the witnesses against Branson. We should keep them all right here together. It'll be easier to watch over everybody. We better get some shut-eye. In a few hours you'll relieve Armstrong upstairs, and I'll take over for Wheeler at the stables."

Jennings carried his rifle into the back room, the sheriff's quarters. Torn hefted some of the wood stacked next to the downstairs stove and carried it up to Armstrong. He and the deputy hauled a bunk out of one of the empty cells and stood it up on end to block the broken window.

After returning to the office, Torn righted the chair and sat with his feet propped up on the desk next to the unconscious Havelock. He was betting that if Hadley tried anything else tonight it would be just before dawn, the best time to catch the enemy by surprise. This was why he wanted to take the second shift.

He fell asleep, chin on chest, arms folded. The Colt Peacemaker in his right hand was pinned against his body by the weight of his left arm. He slept fitfully, haunted by ghosts from his past. . . .

CHAPTER

JUNE 13, 1862.

The squadron swept forward, sun flashing on steel.

They thundered over the brow of a hill. Torn saw the bluecoats then; the federal troops were dismounted, horses held in reserve.

An extraordinary sight captured his attention: a solitary Union officer on horseback, galloping right at the South Carolinians, straight into the teeth of the rebel charge. As the squadron swarmed down the hill, the officer checked his mount so sharply that the horse seemed to sit down in the middle of the road. The man discharged his pistol, wheeled around, and spurred away with the utmost vigor. Torn and his men, many now cutting loose with the fox hunter yell, gave chase.

The thin blue line of dismounted federals fired. The crackling of gunfire was drowned out by the drumroll of horses at full gallop. Torn did not look back to see if anyone had been hit. He sat erect in the saddle, saber drawn and pointed toward the enemy.

The federals fired another ragged volley, then mounted and withdrew. Torn pressed after them. The road crossed Totopotomoy Creek. He expected the bluecoats to make another stand at the bridge and yelled curt orders to Stewart, who led his troops in a flanking movement. While Torn and the remainder of the squadron rode into a wall of gunfire coming from the bridge, Stewart's detachment crashed at breakneck speed through the tangle of underbrush on the creek's bank and splashed across the shallows. Caught by surprise and in fear of being flanked, the federals once more pulled back.

There followed a mad dash through the abandoned streets of Old Church, the South Carolina cavalrymen hot on the heels of the Union horse soldiers.

The sudden arrival of reinforcements encouraged the federals, who abruptly about-faced and charged their relentless pursuers. The road at this point was hemmed in by woods; the columns crashed into one another with a mighty tumult of steel ringing against steel, pistols cracking, men shouting, horses screaming as they collided and went down. Hand-to-hand fighting spilled into the trees.

Torn fought with a cold and savage fury, pistol in one hand, flashing saber in the other, the reins clenched in his teeth. He fired point-blank into one federal's chest, parried a swing from another that would have decapitated him. As the bluecoat rode past, Torn struck back with a saber stroke that cut deeply into the man's shoulder. The federal cried out, slumped forward across the neck of his horse. The current of close combat swept him away before Torn could finish him off.

A Yankee bugle sounded recall. The federals disengaged, fleeing down the road in disorder. Torn took a quick look around. The Union countercharge had caught them by surprise and stopped them cold. His South Carolina boys had outdistanced the rest of Stuart's cavalry and for a time had been outnumbered. Dead and wounded men, blue and gray, were scattered across the roadway and into the trees. Riderless horses milled. Back along the road in the direction of Totopotomoy Creek, Fitz Lee's Virginians were galloping forward in a cloud of dust. Their timely arrival, Torn assumed, was the reason the federals had withdrawn.

Brett Yarnell rode up, standard in one hand, bloody saber in the other. His blood-splattered face—enemy blood, Torn judged—was split by a happy grin.

"Now, that's what I joined up for!" cried Brett.

Stewart arrived. "Do we press on?"

"Do you want the Virginians to take the lead?" Torn fired back, reloading his pistol.

"I'd rather die first!" Brett declared, then spurred his horse forward.

Torn stood in his stirrups. "South Carolina!" he yelled. "Follow me!"

The squadron surged onward, the Virginians hot on their heels.

They reached a clearing and the intersection of the Mechanicsville Turnpike with the road from Old Church. The clearing was filled with tents and wagons in rows. The federals were fleeing eastward; only a handful of stragglers lingered in the camp. Torn's cavalry swept through and made quick work of them.

Torn called off the chase. His men were scattered, their horses exhausted. He ordered the tents and wagons burned. Mules and horses abandoned by the enemy were rounded up. A mob of men around a Yankee ambulance wagon drew his attention, and he rode forward to investigate. A keg of whiskey had been found, causing all the excitement. Torn had the keg confiscated, the ambulance wagon put to the torch.

One of Stuart's aides arrived, requesting Torn's presence at another council of war.

They had a choice, Stuart told his officers. They could go back whence they had come, by way of Hanover Court House, or press boldly forward, wreaking havoc behind McClellan's lines, knowing full well they might be trapped somewhere along the way with no hope of escape. They would be risking everything—it was a hundred-mile ride around the Army of the Potomac.

"The Yankees will expect us to turn back," said Stuart. "They will throw everything they have into Hanover Court House, hoping to intercept us. But we have accomplished our mission. Learned what we came here to learn. Little Mac's right flank is vulnerable. We have found no fortifications. This is what General Lee wished us to ascertain. On the other hand, not far ahead of us lies the York River Railroad, the enemy's main line of supply."

Stuart was asking for their opinions, but Torn sensed the general had already made his decision. The vote to press on was unanimous. Stuart was gratified. Bursting with pride, he gave the orders to march.

The column re-formed, tired men on tired horses. But no one complained, so high were expectations, so grave the danger. Stewart, too rational to look on the bright side, soberly shared with Torn his bleak assessment of their chances.

"It's neck or nothing now, brother. The odds against us are ten to one."

Torn grinned. "Well, we're twelve hundred men surrounded by an army of one hundred twenty thousand. If, as we claim, one of us can whip ten of them, I'd say you're right on the money."

On they rode. The bright morning gave way to a stormy afternoon. The rain came in quick, fierce summer squalls, turning the roads into quagmires. Tennyson's words kept coming back to Torn time and again, as he wondered what lay ahead: "Half a league, half a league, Half a league onward, All in the valley of death Rode the six hundred."

He thought about Melony Hancock, and whether he would ever see her again.

CHAPTER 15

THE CONFEDERATE COLUMN PASSED SMITH'S
Store, crossed the Matadequin. At Garlick's, a land-
ing on the Pamunkey, two Union transport barges
laden with supply wagons were burned. Approaching
Tunstall's Station, and warned by scouts Redmond
Burke and John Mosby that federal infantry guarded
the railroad there, Stuart called up the artillery.

A howitzer became hopelessly stuck in a mudhole.
As Torn passed the struggling gun crew, he quickly
assessed the situation and devised a possible solution. The keg of whiskey captured at Old Church
was set atop the mired field piece.

"Tell your men they can have that keg if they pull
through," he told the sergeant in charge of the hap-
less crew.

The gunners sprang into the mudhole with a

vengeance, ardently eyeing the keg, and with a her-
culean effort literally lifted the howitzer out of the
grasping muck and set it on firmer ground. Passing
cavalrymen laughed and cheered. But Brett Yarnell,
for one, was not amused.

"You gave away our whiskey," he complained, the
picture of dejection.

"You might be thankful for that howitzer somewhere down the road," replied Torn.

"They shoot like drunkards even when they're
sober," groused Brett.

The scouts' reports proved accurate; two companies of bluecoat infantry defended Tunstall's Station. A federal officer could be heard shouting at
Torn's squadron as they emerged from the woodland
road.

"Koom yay! Koom yay!"

"What's he trying to say?" Stewart asked.

"Damn Dutchman," growled Brett. "I think he
wants us to come on in and give ourselves up."

"I've got a better idea," said Torn. "Let's go in
and see if *he'll* give up."

Yelling like Comanches, the squadron charged.
From the edge of the woods behind them came the
distinct bark of the howitzer. A shell screamed over
their heads, exploded right in the center of the federal line. The Yankee soldiers scattered like quail.

"Pretty fair shooting for drunkards," Torn told
Brett.

They drove the bluecoats out of Tunstall's. Torn
set details to work tearing up the rails. Another detachment hurried to the bridge over Black Creek

with the intention of setting the span ablaze. Farley the scout and several troopers took up axes and began chopping down telegraph poles.

A steam whistle's shriek and a plume of black smoke announced the imminent arrival of a train from the east. The rails had not yet been pulled. Torn ordered wagons placed onto the tracks and concealed his men. The train, a locomotive pulling a string of flatcars loaded with federal troops, slowed as it approached the station, but an overanxious rebel fired his weapon too soon, and the trap was sprung.

The engineer threw open the throttle. The locomotive surged forward, smashing the wagons into so much kindling. The Confederates gave chase on horseback. The federals on the flatcars started shooting. A brief but fierce firefight ensued, but the train escaped.

The rebels burned the bridge and tore up the rails. They torched freight cars, full of fodder, which sat idle on sidings. The orange glow of leaping flames mixed with the ruddy light of sunset.

Night fell, but the column moved on. The sky cleared. A bright moon appeared, one day past full. Exhausted troopers slept slumped in their saddles. The federal prisoners, numbering about 150, were mounted on captured mules, two to an animal.

Stuart called a brief halt at Talleysville. The column was strung out, and he wanted it closed up before crossing the Chickahominy. The prevailing sentiment was that if they could get across that river, the worst would be over. Stuart did not want to leave anyone behind.

The Confederates looted the wagons of captured Union sutlers. Delicacies meant for the enemy were consumed by the ravenous rebel troopers: sausages, molasses, cakes, lemons, figs, and crackers. A crate of champagne was discovered. Torn made sure Brett got a bottle, to make up for the keg of whiskey. Popping corks sounded like a fusillade of musket fire.

Talleysville was the site of a federal field hospital. Stuart ordered Torn to post a guard there and to present to the Union doctors his personal guarantee that the Confederates would not touch the facility. Torn learned from one of the surgeons that the hospital—several huge tents covering a meadow a mile west of town—overflowed with wounded and that some patients and supplies had been housed in a nearby plantation home.

Torn arrived at the plantation house in time to intercept four of Hadley Fourcade's troopers coming down the tree-lined drive. Three of the men were mounted; the fourth drove a wagon loaded with crates.

"What do you carry in that wagon, Sergeant?" Torn asked the three-striper in charge of the detail.

"Medical supplies, mostly, Captain. Found 'em in the big house yonder."

The house was partially visible through the trees, gleaming like a chunk of ivory in the moonlight.

"By whose order did you confiscate these supplies?"

Torn's stern tone of voice had the sergeant shifting uncomfortably in his saddle.

"Lieutenant Fourcade, sir. He's still up there, having words with the Yankee doctor. They're not exactly passing the time of day, if you get my meaning, sir."

"Put those supplies back where you found them," snapped Torn. "The wounded have need of them."

"Yes, sir. But, Captain . . . they're Yankees."

"They're men first and foremost. Carry out my order, Sergeant."

"The lieutenant won't like it, sir."

Torn lost his temper. "To hell with the lieutenant and what he likes. Do as I say, mister."

He waited until the sergeant had turned the wagon around before going back to the road leading into Talleysville.

Minutes later the sound of a galloping horse caused him to check his mount and lay hand to saber. The countryside had to be swarming with federals now, all as mad as hornets, and Torn was well aware that the enemy could strike from any direction at any moment.

But this rider wore gray. It was Hadley Fourcade, and he was furious.

"How dare you countermand my orders!" raged Hadley.

"Watch your tone with me, Lieutenant."

Hadley touched the scar on his cheek. "Go to hell."

Torn smiled coldly. "Soldiers don't wage war on the wounded. Only cowards do that."

With a strangled cry of inarticulate fury, Hadley drew his saber. Torn's horse was as surprised as its rider; the animal shied away from Fourcade's violence. Moonlight flashed on steel as Torn swept his own blade from its scabbard. Sabers rang together as he deflected Hadley's swing. Fourcade raked his mount with his spurs. The horse lunged forward, striking Torn's mount broadside. As his horse went down, Torn kicked out of the stirrups and rolled clear. Hadley galloped past, wheeled, and charged. Torn dodged a vicious, arcing swing that could have cut him in two. Again Hadley turned his horse and charged. Again Torn desperately eluded his steel.

"Coward!" screamed Hadley. "Stand and fight like a man!"

He jumped off his horse and charged, this time on foot. Torn rushed to meet him, struck Hadley's saber with his own, driving it downward, slamming his elbow into Hadley's face at the same time. Hadley fell, rolled away from Torn's slashing saber, bounced to his feet, parried a thrust. They circled, dancing to the deadly song of clashing steel. Hack, thrust, parry. Hadley let his rage get the better of him, threw caution to the wind. Torn deflected a wild stroke and stepped in to deliver a punch that sent Fourcade sprawling. He drove the saber from Hadley's grasp with a mighty two-handed swing.

Hadley looked up, and even in the moon-splintered darkness Torn could see the consuming hate blazing in the man's eyes. The breath rasping in his throat, Torn lifted his saber for the killing stroke.

Suddenly his rage abandoned him, leaving him cold and unsure. He hesitated, straddling Hadley, holding the saber high overhead. For some reason, he couldn't kill this man. Even though he knew, had the roles been reversed, Hadley would have killed him without compunction.

He stepped back, lowered the saber.

The sound of horses, the trundle of a wagon, reached his ears. Hadley's troopers, coming from the plantation house.

Hadley got to his feet, grinning like a wolf.

"So go ahead," he sneered. "Put me under arrest. Prefer charges against me. Have your damned court-martial. A firing squad can do what you lack the guts to."

Torn knew he would be well within his rights to do precisely what Hadley had just prescribed. He also knew he couldn't. Bringing the crushing weight of stern military justice to bear on Hadley smacked, somehow, of cowardice. Of employing someone else to fight his fights for him.

The sergeant arrived a little ahead of the troopers. The old three-striper had a nose for trouble, and he smelled some now.

"What's happened here, Captain?"

Looking Hadley square in the eye, Torn said, "Yankee patrol jumped us. They fled into the woods. No point in searching for them now."

One of the troopers brought up his horse. Torn sheathed his saber and mounted.

"Let's get back to the column," he said. "It's close to midnight. We'll be pulling out then. Seven more miles and we're across the Chickahominy."

"And home free," exclaimed the sergeant, awed by the audacity of their accomplishment. "By jiminy, we'll have rid all the way around Little Mac and his bluebellies!"

"We're not out of the fire yet," cautioned Torn.

But he knew the worst was over. He figured the federals were concentrating behind them, between Tunstall's Station and Hanover Court House, expecting Stuart to leave their house by the same door he had used coming in. Now Torn understood that Stuart's bold plan to ride completely around the Army of the Potomac had been their only realistic option all along.

He turned his back on Hadley and rode for Talleysville, wondering when and where Fourcade would try to kill him next.

16

ARMBRUSTER ARRIVED AT THE DOOR OF THE HAR-
risonville jailhouse early in the morning. Armstrong
was up in the cellblock watching Branson. Marshal
Havelock, not quite himself after his ordeal last night,
was laid up in the back room. That left Jennings to
cover from one of the windows, peering through the
shutter gunport, as Torn lifted the bar off the door
and stepped out onto the boardwalk.

"Morning, Mayor."

Armbruster was in no mood for the amenities.
With the appearance of a man about to be violently
sick, he was staring at the four bodies laid out in
front of the jail. The corpses of Spivey and the three
bushwhackers were stiff with rigor mortis. Torn was
able to look at them with detachment—he'd seen
literally thousands of bodies in his time, and that

99

much experience had killed something inside him.

"I've got a couple of men in a wagon down the street, Judge," said Armbruster. "Ready to take these four to the undertaker, if you'll permit it."

Torn glanced south along the main street. He saw the buckboard, the two men. They looked harmless enough. But appearances could be deceiving. Hadley was a wily son with a hatful of tricks. Torn looked north, peering at the livery, particularly the loft door. Wheeler had just relieved him at that post, and though he could not see the deputy, Torn felt confident the man was in place with gun ready.

"Pretty quiet this morning," commented Torn. "Place looks like a ghost town."

"You can take credit for that," Armbruster replied with asperity. "No one dares venture out. The citizens are prisoners in their own homes. Huddled behind locked doors, in fear for their lives."

"Don't you think Hadley Fourcade ought to get some of the credit?"

"I don't approve of Fourcade and his men, and neither do the majority of the people here in Harrisonville. We are peaceful, God-fearing folk, Judge. We mind our own business, and he leaves us alone. But your presence here puts us all in harm's way. You don't know Fourcade. He'll take the entire town to task for harboring you. He could do to Harrisonville what Curtis and his Redlegs did in 'sixty-four."

"What was that?"

"Those Kansas renegades burned a large portion of this town to the ground. I'd truly hate to see that happen again."

"Fourcade can't do that unless you and your people let him."

Armbruster was skeptical. "We're no match for the bushwhackers. We're farmers and merchants. We have our wives and children to think about. Our homes and livelihoods."

"Those are all things worth fighting for. Worth dying for, if need be."

Incredulous, Armbruster emphatically shook his head. "You don't understand."

"You're the one who doesn't understand," Torn replied curtly. "You turn the other cheek to a man like Hadley Fourcade, he'll knock your head off."

Armbruster adamantly refused to concede the point. "You've put us in an impossible situation. I pray that the blood of innocents will not be spilled. If it is, it will be on your hands."

Exasperated, Torn made a gesture of dismissal.

"Go on, call in your men. Bury them quick. I want everybody to attend that town meeting, and I want to hold it this morning."

"I spread the word. Ten o'clock, in the church. But I can't guarantee anyone will show up."

At the mayor's signal, the two men brought the wagon in and loaded up the dead. From the doorway, Torn watched this grim work. As the wagon pulled away with its grisly cargo, he spotted a man approaching on foot. His hand dropped to the Colt Peacemaker on his hip. This reflex agitated Armbruster, already jumpy as a cat.

"No need for that, Judge. It's Thurlow Odom."

"What's a Thurlow Odom?"

The newcomer was advancing like a cavalry charge. His long strides carried him near enough to hear Torn's remark. He saw Torn reach for the Colt, but it did not faze him; he wore an expression of fearless determination as he confronted the judge.

"I happen to be an attorney, sir. A respected member of this community, I might add. I have come here to consult with my client."

"Your client?"

"The man in your custody. Caleb Branson."

Armbruster was fidgeting. The mayor looked as if he had suddenly remembered he was late for an important engagement. "I must go, gentlemen, if you will excuse me."

"You know, Mayor," Torn said, smiling, "I don't recall saying anything about Branson when we spoke last night."

Armbruster blanched and beat a hasty retreat.

"If you please, sir," Odom snapped, superciliously. He was a big man, as tall as Torn and a hundred pounds heavier, but more flab than brawn. Clad in a tailored black broadcloth suit, a white linen shirt, and hand-lasted Jefferson boots, he had a prosperous, well-groomed look about him, and reeked of French quinine. He had a bulldog face, florid and heavy-jowled and belligerent. Stepping left, then right, he sought in vain an opening by which he might outflank Torn and gain entrance into the jailhouse.

"How did you know we had Caleb Branson, Mr. Odom?" Torn was polite but insistent.

"How I came by that information is no concern of yours."

"You intend to represent Branson."

"Did I not say he was my client?"

"You're pretty well informed, Mr. Odom. I guess you know why Branson is in federal custody as well."

Odom opened his mouth to respond, clamped it shut, and eyed Torn suspiciously. "I trust I will be acquainted with the charges, in time." He made a production of consulting his watch, depended on a Dickens chain hooked to a buttonhole in his vest. "Now, sir, unless you intend to deny Mr. Branson his right to counsel, I would like to proceed."

"You'll make better progress when you climb down off that high horse," predicted Torn.

Odom abruptly abandoned the bluster and intimidation. "I've heard about you, Judge. Oh, yes, I've heard all the stories they tell. You're a hard man, they say, but fair. I'm sure we both want to see that Branson gets a fair trial. We are both committed to a high ideal—that the law be as just as it is impartial."

Torn got his first good read of the man at that moment. Odom's deft change of tactics revealed him to be a cagey character. One it would be unwise to underestimate.

Wearing a counterfeit smile, Torn stepped aside and motioned for Odom to enter the jail.

The attorney fired a disdainful glance at Jennings and steered a course for the staircase. Obviously he knew his way around; no doubt many of his clients had been guests at this establishment. He gave little attention to the charred section of floor or the bloodstains that were just about everywhere.

"Not so fast," said Torn, closing and barring the

door. "We'll have to check you for weapons."

"Surely my word as a gentleman will suffice."

"Would that be a southern gentleman, by any chance?"

"You say that in a snide way. As a matter of fact, I am. And I was given to understand that you were, too."

"I used to be. Hadley Fourcade used to be. But, gentleman or not, Jennings here is going to search you."

Odom waxed indignant. "This is an outrage! I protest most strongly, sir. I . . . Have a care!"

This last was directed at Jennings, who was frisking Odom with the thoroughness of a highwayman. He lightened the lawyer's load to the tune of one .38 caliber pocket pistol.

"Huh," grunted Jennings, looking askance at the gun. "One of them newfangled five-shots by Hopkins and Allen. Imagine that." He grinned at Odom. "This here peashooter's such a lightweight, I reckon you must've just forgot you were hauling it around."

Odom's cheeks were mottled with unbecoming spots of crimson. He was both infuriated and embarrassed.

"So much for southern gentlemen," murmured Torn.

He escorted the lawyer upstairs.

"Hadley sent you a present, Branson," he said.

Odom glowered, tight-lipped.

Branson came to the cell door. He stuck his arms through the strap iron and just seemed to hang there, an indolent pose, as befitted a man who was trying to impress everyone with his unruffled cool. Odom took a step closer to the cell; Torn's grip was like an iron vise on his shoulder, restraining him from taking a second.

"That's close enough," said Torn. "That man over there with the scattergun is a deputy marshal." Armstrong touched the brim of hat and smiled lazily. "He's going to stay up here while you two have your little chat. If you get any closer to the prisoner, Mr. Odom, or if the deputy sees anything passed between you, he's going to unload both barrels."

"You can't do this," Odom protested. "My conversation with my client should be confidential."

"Fine. Don't listen, Armstrong."

"This is a farce!" cried Odom. "You've already subjected me to the indignity of a search. Now this."

Someone was tapping on the door downstairs. "That's the way it's going to be," Torn told the lawyer as he turned to leave the cellblock. "Take it or leave it."

He descended to the office. Jennings was looking through the gunport at the front window. "One man," he reported. "Doesn't seem to be heeled, but he could have a hideout."

Prepared for trouble, Torn opened the door.

A gaunt man confronted him. He wore a felt eyeshade and sleeve garters. His features were birdlike, nervous.

"You the marshal?"

"Judge."

The man threw hasty looks up and down the empty street.

"Reckon I ought not to be here. Ought to mind my own business. Edna's always telling me to. Edna's my wife."

"Congratulations. Who are you?"

"Oh. Sorry. Name's Jared. Jared Calkins. I'm the telegrapher. Office down at the depot, you know. What I come for, I thought you ought to know."

Torn waited, then asked, "Know what?"

"The westbound train."

"What about it?"

"It was due in an hour ago."

"That the only train coming in today?"

"Only one," confirmed Calkins.

Torn grimaced. It had to be the train carrying the prosecutor, Cooke, and the two witnesses against Branson.

"The train ever come in late?"

"Not an hour late. Not unless there's trouble. Something else you ought to know."

Again Torn waited, and again he had to prompt Calkins. "What?"

"Seems to me the telegraph line is down somewhere twixt here and Warrensburg." Calkins apprehensively checked the street once more. "Just thought you ought to know, is all. Not that I'm taking sides. I don't take sides. Edna says never take sides, and I . . ."

Torn closed the door.

"You look like a man with a bad gut hunch," observed Jennings.

"You and Armstrong and the marshal will have to

hold it down here," said Torn. "I'm going to take Wheeler and find that train. If we lose those witnesses, our bacon's in the fire."

"I thought it already was," remarked Jennings.

CHAPTER 17

TORN AND WHEELER FOLLOWED THE TRACKS OF the Pacific Railroad eastward out of Harrisonville. They made fairly good time, though the snow was deep. As the morning progressed, an ominous rank of gray-black storm clouds marched over the northern horizon and advanced relentlessly. Torn knew a blizzard when he saw one. He hoped they would not have to go far to solve the mystery of the missing train, as he did not care to be caught out in the open when a blue norther came through. In his years as a frontier judge he had witnessed a few truly fearsome winter storms. He'd seen trees split open by the cold, cattle frozen upright in their tracks. And it was plenty cold to suit him even now, with the sun shining. He wore Havelock's mackinaw coat. His greatcoat was ruined—the jailhouse fire had burned holes in it.

A couple of hours out of town they spotted a plume of smoke rising a mile or so ahead. It did not have the form or appearance of the smoke that came from a locomotive's diamond stack. They rode on, listening tensely for the sound of gunfire.

Torn assumed that if Hadley had ambushed the train, he'd have brought plenty of bushwhackers along with him to get the job done right. If that was the case, Torn had to wonder how much he and one U.S. deputy marshal could accomplish—beyond getting themselves killed.

But they heard no shooting. The snowbound countryside was as hushed as a church come Monday morning. Before long they had the train in sight. The Jupiter locomotive had been derailed. Its front end was buried in the snow. Steam and smoke rose from the boiler. The tender stood across the tracks at right angles to the mogul. Blocks of wood were scattered for a hundred yards in every direction, testimony to the violence of the wreck. Two day coaches, three boxcars, and a caboose remained more or less on the rails. Many of the windows in the day coaches had been shattered. Assessing the extent of the damage, Torn deduced that the engineer had seen the break in the iron in time to begin slowing the train. In so doing, the railroader had averted a tragedy of potentially much greater dimensions.

A dozen people were milling around on both sides of the train. A few more stood near a clump of trees fifty yards south of the track. Torn could see three bodies dangling from a stout limb. He steered his horse in that direction, Wheeler in tow. The deputy pointed out the telegraph lines that had been cut and now dangled from one of the poles that paralleled the rails. Torn nodded grimly and rode on.

A hue and cry arose from the people near the train. Torn assumed they were passengers and crew— that the bushwhackers had long since departed— and he considered the possibility that this spooked bunch of victims might conceivably mistake him and Wheeler for outlaws.

Just then a pistol barked.

"Hold your fire!" he yelled, sharply checking his horse.

The pistol spoke again. Torn took small consolation in the fact that the range was a little long for a side gun.

Wheeler cursed softly. "Damn fools."

"They've had a bad day," said Torn, surprised by his own tolerance.

He pulled a spare shirt out of his saddlebags and waved it overhead.

"Are we surrendering?" Wheeler asked dryly.

"I did that once," Torn replied with grim humor, "and regretted it for sixteen months thereafter."

Surrender or not, the tactic worked. It stopped the shooting, which came from the group near the train. Torn and Wheeler proceeded to the trees.

"God Almighty," muttered Wheeler.

It was not a pretty sight.

The three men standing nearby slogged over through deep snow. One of them wore the garb of a railroader. All of them looked as if they'd lost their breakfast or were about to. It was the railroader who spoke first.

"You men from Harrisonville?"

"Clay Torn, federal judge. This man is a deputy marshal."

The railroader nodded sideways at the three corpses decorating the tree.

"There was nothing we could do. Too many bush-whackers."

"Damned butchers," grumbled one of the others, both of whom Torn assumed were passengers.

"Must've been twenty or thirty of them, all told," continued the railroader. "Probably pulled up the rails last night, then sat back and waited for us to come through. Knew our schedule, because we rolled through here right before dawn. They were on us before we saw them. The engineer and fireman are bad hurt. So are a few of the passengers. The bush-whackers pulled these three poor devils off the train, dragged them over here, and strung them up. Then they doused the bodies with kerosene and set them on fire."

One of the charred hanging ropes snapped, drop-ping a still-smoldering corpse into the snow. The sickly sweet stench of burned flesh reached Torn.

"Why did they burn 'em?" asked Wheeler, shaken.

"Scare tactic," replied Torn. "They're trying to rattle us."

Wheeler drew a ragged breath. "Is it Cooke and the witnesses?"

"What do you think?" snapped Torn. "How long

ago did they ride out?" he asked the railroader.

"Less than a half hour. Headed north. Look, Judge, we've got a problem. A storm's coming, and my knees tell me it's going to be god-awful."

"Your knees?" echoed Wheeler, bewildered.

"Yeah. My knees get to aching something fierce every time bad weather's in the offing. Point is, we've got injured people here. Now, it's ten miles to Harrisonville that way, and twenty back to Warrensburg the other. This train isn't going anywhere, and the telegraph's been cut. What do we do?"

Torn had already put his mind to that problem.

"Wheeler here will ride to Warrensburg and get help, bring another train out to pick you people up. It'll be five hours there, an hour or so to get back. In the meantime, you get everybody into one of the day coaches. Gather up plenty of wood to keep the stove stoked."

"Harrisonville's closer. If we could get a few wagons out here . . ."

Torn shook his head. "Not in this snow. Besides, Harrisonville is the last place you or any of these people want to be."

"What's going on here?" asked the railroader.

"You just worry about your passengers."

"Wait a minute," said one of the other men. "I've got business in Harrisonville."

"You'd do well to take my advice," said Torn. "Because if you go to Harrisonville, you might end up doing business with the undertaker."

CHAPTER 18

TORN RODE TO THE TRAIN, INTENDING TO CHECK on the wounded. Riding alongside, Wheeler said, "I don't cotton much to the idea of leaving you and the others, Judge. Looks to me like you'll be needing every gun."

"These people need help. Besides, I'll expect you back in Harrisonville with reinforcements by tomorrow."

Wheeler was silent a moment. "That might be too late."

"We'll know that tomorrow."

The people around the train were relieved to learn that Torn and Wheeler were the law. They looked plenty scared, and Torn could hardly blame them. One man apologized sheepishly for shooting at them. Another complained that the bushwhackers had robbed him blind. Torn smiled grimly at this news. Hadley's men might claim they fought for a noble cause and had ambushed the train with murder on their minds, but they hadn't let the opportunity for a little larceny pass them by.

A woman had emerged from one of the day coaches to see what the shooting was about. She now stood on the platform rocking a crying infant in her arms. Silent tears streaked the woman's cheeks. The sight filled Torn with cold fury. Hadley was up to his old tricks, waging war on the defenseless. So much for the gentleman's code of honor.

The conductor pushed through the throng closing in around Torn and the deputy, and Torn advised him to move everybody into one of the day coaches, explaining briefly that Wheeler would ride to Warrensburg for a rescue train. He asked about the condition of the wounded. The conductor assured him that all the passengers hurt in the derailment had suffered only minor injuries. The same could not be said for the engineer and the fire stoker. These men were still in the Jupiter locomotive.

Torn found the injured railroaders laid out on the locomotive's iron apron, covered with blankets. Steam hissed from a cracked valve on the boiler. A young man in city clothes was tying a splint to the arm of one of the wounded. A young woman ministered to the other, who appeared to be in the worst shape. He'd received an ugly gash along the hairline. Like all head wounds, this one bled profusely. The woman was calmly and skillfully sewing up the gash with a needle and thread.

"Can they be moved into one of the coaches?" asked Torn.

"It might be dangerous," said the woman. "I don't know how badly they are hurt. There might be internal injuries. But I suppose we must do it. In their weakened condition, how much of this cold can they withstand? First, though, let me finish here. This poor man has lost a great deal of blood."

"Are you a nurse?"

"No. A schoolteacher."

She was extremely attractive, with tawny hair and bottle green eyes. Her features and complexion were perfect. Torn admired her composure most of all. Her hands were covered with the man's blood. As she brushed a stray tendril of hair out of her eyes, she left a scarlet smear on her forehead. But she didn't seem at all squeamish.

Wheeler and the young man, who introduced himself as a mail-order salesman, carried the other injured railroader to the day coach. Torn waited and watched while the woman finished her stitching. Only when she was done did she let her carefully maintained composure slip, revealing the strain and weariness. She sat back on her heels, shivering slightly from the cold. A blustery wind was sweeping down from the north in advance of the fast-moving line of clouds. She closed her eyes a moment. They snapped open as Torn draped his borrowed mackinaw coat around her shoulders.

"Why did you do that?" she asked.

The query surprised him; the answer was obvious.

"Because you're cold. You'd best get back to the

day coach with the others." He told her his plan to rescue the stranded crew and passengers.

"I'm going to Harrisonville," she declared.

"That's not a good idea."

"I must go," she insisted. "You can't prevent me from going."

He was impressed by everything about her. She had looks, courage, spirit.

"You could be in danger," he said. "We're about to have a war in Harrisonville."

"I'm going," she repeated. She stood and climbed down out of the Jupiter. He watched as she washed the blood off her hands with snow.

"I hope you'll listen to reason," he said. "I'd be concerned for your safety, Miss . . ."

"Branson. Kate Branson."

He stared. "Caleb Branson's sister?"

"Yes. And you . . . Might you be the marshal who took my brother to Harrisonville for trial?"

"I'm a federal judge. Clay Torn, at your service, ma'am."

He braced for a display of malice from Kate Branson. But she surprised him again with a smile that was genuine, if a little sad.

"I warned Caleb something like this would happen. I told him that sooner or later he would have to answer to the law. And now here you are. The law." Her gaze swept the length of the wrecked train. Anger quirked the corners of her mouth. "I hope and pray you can stop the bushwhackers, Judge. This kind of thing simply can't be allowed to continue. Innocent people terrorized." She looked toward the trees, where two of the three hanged men turned slowly in the wind. "And murdered."

Wheeler and the young salesman returned to carry the second railroader back to the day coach.

"I take it," said Torn, "that you were going to Harrisonville to see your brother."

"I *am* going. I never approved of what he did. Not that he told me anything. He tried to make me believe he was employed as a gun guard for an express company. Isn't that ironic? But I knew. He never was able to lie to me. We've always been very close. Our parents died when we were young. He's the only kin I have left. I must see him. One last time, before you hang him."

"How did you know he was in Harrisonville? Moving him from Gratiot Prison was supposed to be a secret. Although," he added wryly, "almost everyone seemed to know about it."

"I found a note on my door a few days ago. It wasn't signed. All it said was that Caleb would be taken to Harrisonville to stand trial for murder. I suppose one of his outlaw associates delivered it in the dead of night. I wouldn't think they'd be so considerate."

Torn pondered this new development. If Kate was telling the truth—and he was disposed to believe she was—then why had Fourcade gone to the trouble of notifying her of her brother's situation? What ulterior motive did he have? Had he done it out of the goodness of his heart? Torn seriously doubted that.

Something else bothered him. Hadley had known

about Branson's transfer to Harrisonville days ago, possibly before Branson had even left the prison in St. Louis. He hadn't needed a spy stationed somewhere along the railroad to tell him, after all.

Wheeler rode up.

"Judge, I'm ready to go."

Torn nodded. "Good luck. I'll see you tomorrow."

"I'll be there," Wheeler vowed. "I don't want to miss *this* war."

He wheeled his horse and galloped east, churning up the snow. As he watched Wheeler go, Torn became aware of Kate Branson's intense gaze.

"You're going back to Harrisonville," she said. "Take me with you."

"Look, Miss Branson . . ."

"I'm going even if I have to walk."

Torn was convinced this was no idle threat.

"We'll have to ride double," he said.

"That won't bother me. Will it you?"

"This is against my better judgment."

"I'll be safer with you than on my own," she said, smiling. "That's what you're thinking. I'm thinking the same thing."

"If we run into bushwhackers, you might change your mind. They could kill you just because you're with me."

"I'll take the chance. You can't talk me out of it, Judge."

"I'm beginning to see that." Torn sighed.

C·H·A·P·T·E·R

19

THEY WERE HALFWAY TO HARRISONVILLE WHEN the bushwhackers struck.

The attack caught Torn by surprise. For once his guard was down. Kate Branson was riding double with him, and the distinct sensation, the seductive warmth, of a woman sharing his saddle brought back a rush of memories. Poignant recollections of a time when he and Melony Hancock had done this very thing, one day months before the outbreak of war, when they'd gone riding and her horse had thrown a shoe. It was a day that seemed both remote and vivid; yesterday and a hundred years ago. Another life, another world, a time of innocence now lost, of contentment all too rare.

The memories of Melony were painful, but Torn was willing to endure the pain; aside from a few old letters and the daguerreotype in the pocket of his frock coat, memories were all he had left.

And so, in a sense, he was daydreaming when the riders surged out of a draw a hundred yards away and started shooting. Five men, fanning out, their mounts laboring at a gallop through deep snow, trailing gun smoke, long coats flapping, and pistols spitting flame.

"Hold tight!" yelled Torn, jerking rein and kicking the dun gelding into a lunging gallop.

Kate wrapped her arms tightly around him. He felt her warm breath on the back of his neck, her breasts pressing against him, and he experienced a tingling down his spine that was completely unassociated with the peril in which they suddenly found themselves. It was right odd, he mused, to have such feelings when five desperadoes were hell-for-leather on his heels and dedicated to the proposition that this would be his last day above snakes.

The dun gelding was a game animal. Grunting with exertion, hot breath steaming from flared nostrils, it plunged through the deep snow. Gunshots—a sound like dry wood splintering—were shredded by the swirling wind. Torn did not bother returning fire. That would have been a waste of both time and ammunition. Rather, he concentrated on urging every iota of speed out of the dun, aiming for a hollow filled with snow-cloaked pines.

The ground fell away, sloping steeply. The dun's back end dropped as it fought for purchase in loose snow that came up to the stirrups. For a moment they were out of sight of the bushwhackers. The gunfire diminished—these men weren't the type to shoot unless they had something to shoot at. Torn drew the Winchester .44–40 out of its saddle boot, swung his right leg over the dun's neck, and jumped clear. He held on to the reins. The dun plunged onward, yanking Torn off his feet. He pulled on the leathers, his weight like an anchor, slowing the horse. Torn held on until Kate had dismounted. She sank almost to her waist in the powder. Torn released the reins, hooked an arm around hers, and started for the nearby trees, high-stepping.

The shooting resumed. Bullets kicked up snow to left and right. Kate stumbled and fell. Torn whirled, brought the Winchester to shoulder, and fired three rounds in rapid succession. The bushwhackers were skylined at the top of the slope, black shapes against the backdrop of a dark and angry winter sky. One man twisted violently in the saddle, toppled sideways. The others pulled up, expecting to shoot it out. Torn disappointed them. Kate was up and running again, so he turned and followed, shielding her as much as he could.

They reached the rim of the trees. Bullets smacked into the trunks of the pines, showering bark shrapnel. Torn's hopes rose. Out in the open, five-to-one odds were too steep; from cover he thought he could give a good accounting of himself. But then Kate cried out and fell, and his heart sank, for he knew she'd been shot even before he saw the blood on the hem of her skirt and on her kid and cloth shoe.

"Just a little farther," he coaxed. "See those rocks?"

Deeper in the trees stood an outcropping of gray granite. She nodded, biting her lip until it bled, but she did not cry out again, and Torn was greatly impressed. With his help she made it to the rocks. He found shelter for her where one massive slab of granite leaned against another, forming an open-ended cavity just large enough to accommodate her. With Kate tucked away, Torn found cover nearby and began shooting back at their pursuers.

The bushwhackers dismounted at the edge of the trees and spread out. One darted from tree to tree, and the angle of his run made Torn suspect him of trying to circle around behind. The other three came straight on, laying down heavy fire. With cool deliberation, Torn fixed his attention on the flanker, put the Winchester's sights on him, led him a hair, and squeezed the trigger as he came out from behind one of the pines. The bushwhacker cartwheeled and lay death-still in the snow.

Torn swung the rifle at the head-on charge of the other three. He fired as fast as he could work the Winchester's action. The three men dived for cover. Torn ducked down behind the rocks.

The shooting diminished. Torn figured they were reloading, maybe talking it over. Would they withdraw, now that two of their number were casualties? Torn doubted it. Whatever else these men were, they weren't the type to give up easily.

With only a couple of rounds left in the Winchester, Torn laid the rifle aside and drew the Colt Peacemaker. A piercing rebel yell made him jump. A hail of hot lead screamed off the rocks all around him.

He crawled to his left, peered through a crevice in the rocks, and saw the three bushwhackers charging again. Brave fools, he thought. Long on gumption, short on sense.

They were shooting fast and furiously, trying to keep him down. But he was no longer where they thought him to be, and when he came up with the Colt blazing, he nailed one squarely in the chest and dropped another, gutshot, before they could turn their guns on his new position. The last man veered away sharply and made a diving leap behind a log, chased by Torn's bullets.

Torn hunkered down again and reloaded the Peacemaker.

"Don't shoot!" yelled the bushwhacker. "I give up! I'm hit!"

Like hell you are, thought Torn, smirking. He did not respond.

Thirty feet away, the gutshot man thrashed in the snow, making grim animal noises. Torn was no longer worried about that one. He would bleed to death in a matter of minutes.

"Hey!" yelled the bushwhacker hiding behind the log. "I'm bad hurt, mister! I'm giving up!"

Torn knew better. The man was trying to draw him out.

The Colt reloaded, Torn climbed higher into the jumble of granite boulders. He found a loose rock that weighed about five pounds, heaved back, and let fly. The rock struck the log at one end with a loud thump. The bushwhacker rose up, spinning and shooting at the sound, thinking it was made by Torn trying to outflank him. From up in the rocks, Torn fired twice. The first bullet struck the man in the side, and the second was a head shot. The outlaw fell backward into blood-splattered snow.

Torn climbed down and checked on Kate, curled in her stony burrow.

"Is it over?" she asked.

"Stay right there," he cautioned, and went out to make certain.

Four of the bushwhackers were dead. The gutshot man was just this side of it. Torn thumbed back the Colt's hammer. The sound turned the bushwhacker's head. Through bleary eyes, he looked at the gun, at Torn's grim countenance.

"It's up to you," said Torn.

The bushwhacker stared for what seemed to Torn a small eternity. He knew, as did Torn, that there was no hope for him. He was dying a slow, lingering death, and Torn was willing to put him out of his misery. The man smiled wanly. Blood leaked from his mouth. He nodded, closed his eyes.

Steeling himself, Torn pulled the trigger, and turned quickly away.

20

HE CAUGHT UP THE DUN GELDING, RETURNED TO the granite outcropping. The wind was howling like a regiment of banshees, whipping the pines into a frenzy.

"We've got to get moving," he told Kate.

She crawled out from beneath the boulder tent, pale and shuddering violently. Torn knew it wasn't just the bitter cold affecting her. From experience, he knew how the human body reacted to the trauma of a gunshot wound.

Mumbling an apology, he lifted her skirt enough to see the blue-black bullet hole in the calf of her right leg. Turning the leg gently, he was relieved to find that the bullet had passed clean through.

"I've got to stop the bleeding," he said.

"Go ahead," she whispered.

The wound needed to be cleaned and cauterized, but he sensed that time was running out. The storm was imminent, and they were several miles from Harrisonville. Their chances of surviving a severe blizzard out here in the open were too poor to contemplate. So he settled for binding the wound tightly with strips torn from the bottom of her petticoat.

Helping her into the saddle, he led the dun gelding out of the hollow and had just reached the railroad tracks when the first gentle flakes of wind-tossed snow began to fall.

Thirty minutes later the world was a frozen hell.

Snow mixed with sleet fell with a vengeance. The temperature plummeted. Cold wind sliced into Torn's eyes, making him weep. His tears turned instantly into ice. He could scarcely see an arm's length in front of him, but kept tenaciously to the tracks, feeling his way inch by inch, sometimes stumbling on the rails and ties.

He figured the railroad was his only chance. If he strayed from it, they were lost, in more ways than one. In a blizzard, a man could go around in circles and remain convinced until the bitter end that he had walked a true course. It was said that this happened because most people were heavier on one side than the other and would veer to the heavy side if deprived of sight. If a man faced a tree a hundred yards away, closed his eyes, and tried to walk straight for it, he would end up at least twenty feet to one side or the other of the tree.

Torn clutched the cheek strap of the dun's bridle, afraid that if he lost his grip on the horse he would lose Kate and never be able to find her again. Now and again he reached back, groping blindly, to make sure she was still astride the gelding.

The shrieking wind cut through him like a steel blade honed to razor sharpness, numbing him to the marrow. His lungs burned. He lost all feeling in his limbs. He concentrated on taking one step at a time. Every step took its toll. The gusts—forty or fifty miles an hour, he guessed—threatened to knock him down, and he leaned heavily into them, tottering like a town drunk, for in a blizzard the wind raged like a lunatic, striking from one direction and then, without warning, from another. To stay upright, to keep moving, was the supreme exertion, and it quickly sucked the strength right out of him.

The dun was frightened and often balked, and Torn had to summon every last ounce of reserve stamina just to get the animal moving again. He suffered, and when he was sick to death of the suffering, he clenched his violently chattering teeth and suffered some more. He did it, mostly, for Kate. When he had gone past the point he felt capable of reaching for his own sake, he went on for her.

Ever so slowly, a seductive warmth crept over him, and when he no longer acknowledged the cold, he became drowsy. He wanted to lie down and go to sleep. He had never wanted anything so badly. It was all he could do to stay on his feet. Instinct kept him going, even as his befuddled mind screamed for rest.

He stumbled, dropped to his knees.

Get up.

"I can't," he mumbled. He couldn't even keep his eyes open.

Get up!

Suddenly he understood.

He was freezing to death.

The realization jolted him, gave him an extra measure of strength, and he got to his feet, kept moving. He resolved to count his steps, but he lost count time after time and was constantly starting over. In desperation, he resorted to punching himself in the face, but no matter how hard he hit, he didn't feel a thing. The deadly warmth kept trying to seduce him, drag him down. More than once he fell asleep in midstride, then jerked awake as his knees buckled and he began to fall. Trying to remain conscious became far more agonizing than the subzero cold.

Despair worked its evil magic to undermine his resolve. What was the point of all this suffering? He couldn't make it. He and Kate were as good as dead. Come spring, maybe, someone would find their bones, picked clean by wolves. Where was the need for a judge now, anyway? The prosecutor was dead. The witnesses were dead. There wasn't going to be any trial. Hadley had won. Torn couldn't make it.

Hadley.

"The hell I can't," Torn muttered.

He could imagine Hadley Fourcade grinning like the devil himself, stroking the scar on his cheek, laughing softly at the news of Clay Torn's death.

The image stoked embers of hate down deep inside Torn, and the heat from those embers gave him new strength. He would stay alive, if only to spite

Hadley. He leaned into the wind and toiled doggedly through the snow, fighting the blizzard, angry at the storm for conspiring with his lifelong enemy, snarling incoherently at the wind, cursing Hadley.

I've been through hell before. I spent sixteen months in hell, thanks to you, Hadley. Damn you, Hadley, I'm coming to get you, you son of a bitch. This storm can't stop me. We're going to settle this once and for all. . . .

Abruptly the wind subsided, the snowfall lessened, and he could see, dimly, buildings ahead in the gray gloom.

Harrisonville.

Lamplight beckoned from a few iced-over windows. Man-high drifts of new snow were piled up against the walls, and foot-long icicles decorated the eaves. The wind shredded woodsmoke rising from dozens of chimneys.

Torn looked back at Kate. She was clinging to the saddle horn with both hands and rode slumped forward. For one frightful instant he thought she was dead. He grabbed her arm, shook it.

"Kate. Kate, we made it."

Slowly, slowly, she raised her head, as though it took tremendous effort, and stared blankly at the town.

Torn continued along the tracks, turned onto the main street. Now that the ordeal was over, exhaustion consumed him. He shuffled along without the strength to lift his feet.

He stopped in front of the jailhouse, pried his stiff fingers from the cheek strap of the dun's bridle, and tried to help Kate down off the horse. She tumbled out of the saddle, and they sprawled in the snow. Torn just wanted to lie there. The mere thought of trying to get up, of taking one more step, appalled him. But he did it anyway, hauling Kate to the door of the jailhouse, pounding on the heavy timbers with his fist.

The door flew open.

"Well, look what the cat dragged in," said Hadley Fourcade, grinning like the devil himself.

CHAPTER 21

MORE THAN TEN YEARS HAD PASSED SINCE TORN
had laid eyes on Hadley Fourcade. The man hadn't
changed much. His face was still dark and angular,
his mouth wide and cruel, the nose aquiline. He still
sported a thin black mustache. His eyes were deep
green and piercing. Raven black hair was combed
back from a widow's peak, with a dusting of gray at
the temples. He looked as dark and dangerous as
ever, especially with that rosette of scar tissue on
the hard brown plane of his cheek, where Torn's
pistol shot had exited.

"Come in out of the weather, Clay," said Hadley.
"We've been waiting for you."

Behind Fourcade stood a half dozen men—grim,
sharp-featured hombres armed to the teeth. Most
of them held pistols aimed in Torn's direction. So did

Hadley, an old Starr Army .44. Torn wondered how many men Fourcade had murdered with this big Civil War–vintage percussion thumb-buster. What he didn't have to speculate about was whether Hadley would use the Starr right here and now if he tried something stupid.

He really didn't have any choice but to accept Hadley's offer, with the blizzard howling at his back and a passel of mean-eyed bushwhackers in his face, so he opted for stepping compliantly into the jailhouse, supporting the semiconscious Kate Branson. Hadley kicked the door shut, but didn't drop the crossbar. Torn noticed little things like that. Sometimes they spelled the difference between life and death.

"Kate!"

Bootheels hammered the stairs as Caleb Branson rushed headlong from the cellblock.

Torn relinquished Kate into Caleb's arms.

"She's been shot," he said.

Branson fired a murderous look at him.

"By one of your colleagues," added Torn. "In the leg. It isn't serious, but it might become so if it isn't tended to."

"Take her into the back room, Caleb," said Hadley. "I'll send someone after the doctor."

Branson gave Hadley a long look, his expression unreadable. There was nothing happy-go-lucky about his demeanor now. He carried his sister into the quarters of the late Sheriff Spivey.

"Tucker, take Clay's horse to the livery, then roust the local sawbones."

One of the bushwhackers departed to do Hadley's bidding. That left five, plus Fourcade. Torn noticed how they were spread out across the room, careful not to bunch up, watching him alertly. Were there any more upstairs in the cellblock? Torn decided it would be smart to assume so.

"Go ahead," said Hadley, reading his mind. "You always did like to play the hero, Clay. Either hand over that handsome new Colt charcoal-burner or use it."

Torn reached slowly across his body and with his left hand removed the Peacemaker from its holster. He offered the gun to Fourcade, butt first.

"You wouldn't pull one of those fancy border rolls on me, would you, Clay?"

"When I kill you, Hadley, there won't be anything fancy about it."

"Bold talk from a dead man." Hadley took the Colt, tossed it on the desk. "Now that big knife of yours. Maybe you were hoping I wouldn't know about that." With the barrel of the Starr he nudged Torn's frock coat open enough to see the saber-knife in its shoulder rig. "Well, I've heard plenty about you over the years. And when they speak of the exploits of Clay Torn, the subject of that knife comes up more often than not."

Torn eased the thong off the saber-knife's pommel. The weapon dropped into his hand. A crazy notion entered his head: one quick, savage stroke, and he could decapitate Hadley. Suicide, of course, but he thought it might almost be worth the price.

Almost.

He handed the saber-knife to Fourcade. Hadley admired it, stuck it under his belt.

"This will give me something to remember you by," he said, and touched the scar on his cheek. "Something besides this. I guess you must be wondering where that marshal and his deputies are. We had to kill one of them. He tried to be a hero. You know what happens to heroes, Clay."

"How would you know?"

"The others are upstairs. Why don't you join them? Cobb, Ruston, escort the good judge to his cell."

One of the bushwhackers clapped a hand on Torn's shoulder. Torn shrugged it off.

"I don't need to be led. I know the way. So keep your hands off me."

Hadley chuckled. "Ease off, Cobb. Clay here is a high and mighty gentleman, and we must treat him accordingly. Just remember, Clay. Pride goes before the fall."

"There you go again, Hadley. Talking about things you know nothing about."

Something lurid and unsafe swirled in Hadley's eyes.

"Don't try to nettle me, old friend."

"You haven't done anything to be proud of since the day you were born."

"You've got some gall," snapped Hadley. "Talking to me about pride. You, a traitor to the Cause. A Yankee judge now." He shook his head. "I never liked you, but I never dreamed you'd be working for the enemy, the invaders of our homeland."

Torn laughed in his face. "If you're going to tell me you're still fighting for the Confederacy, save your breath."

"Get him out of here," growled Fourcade.

The two bushwhackers hauled Torn upstairs to the cellblock. Another outlaw stood guard over Havelock and Armstrong, who occupied the cell that had once confined Caleb Branson. Torn was thrown into the adjacent cell.

"So it was Jennings," said Torn.

Havelock nodded grimly. He sat on the narrow bunk. His shoulder was tightly dressed, the arm in a bandanna sling. Armstrong was hunkered down in a corner, coldly watching the guard. Torn noticed the bushwhacker was carrying Armstrong's scattergun. The deputy looked as though all he wanted was half a chance at getting his property back.

"It was that damned lawyer, Odom," growled Havelock. He had the look of a grizzly bear with a toothache. "By the way, where's my coat? It's as cold as a horse trader's handshake up here."

"I lent it to a lady. What about Odom? He killed Jennings?"

"He had a hand in it. Came by this morning, knocked on the door. Jennings opened up. Didn't see anybody else out there. They were waiting in the alley. When the door opened, Odom kept Jennings from getting the door closed. I was coming out of the back room when I saw that bastard Fourcade shoot Jennings point-blank in the head. That pack of hyenas stuck their hoglegs in my teeth. Nothing I could do."

"Sorry, Marshal. I know Jennings was a friend."

"Damned right. Les and I go back a ways. He was a man to ride the river with, and that's a double-certified fact. What lady?"

"Caleb Branson's sister."

Havelock's jaw dropped.

"You gave my coat to a bushwhacker's sister? Whose side are you on, Torn?"

"You're still singing that old song? You see me locked up in here, don't you?"

"How did you meet up with Branson's sister?"

"It's a long story," said Torn. He began to shed his clothes, which were soggy with melted ice and snow.

"Where's Wheeler?"

"I'll tell you later." Torn threw a meaningful glance at the guard.

Havelock got the message: Torn didn't care to talk about Wheeler with a bushwhacker eavesdropping.

"What are you doing?" asked the marshal. "You'll freeze your *cojones* off."

Torn pulled the blanket off his bunk and toweled himself dry. He rubbed vigorously, and the coarse wool chafed his skin, but it brought feeling back into his arms and legs. His body dry, he sat on the bunk and used the blanket to wipe his clothes off.

"What about Cooke?" Havelock pressed. "The witnesses?"

Torn's smile was thin and humorless. "You don't still think we're going to have a trial, do you?"

"Fourcade and his murdering scum curled their toes, didn't they?"

"Permanently."

"Wonder why they haven't done us the same favor?"

"They'll get around to it," said Torn.

"That's right," seconded the guard, stepping forward with an unpleasant leer plastered across his face. "We're aiming to do to you what you would've done to Caleb. Heard Hadley say so his own self. We're going to hang you boys. You'll all dance at the end of a rope. Then we'll set your stinking Yankee carcasses on fire, just like we done them fellers we pulled off that train."

"Get back over there where you were," Havelock said contemptuously. "You smell like dog droppings."

"I'll take pleasure watching you swing, you bastard," said the guard. "Tomorrow morning. Better say your prayers."

He walked off. Torn put his damp clothes back on, stretched out on the bunk, and groaned. Every joint and muscle ached. He covered up with the blanket. It was cold in the cellblock, but nothing like the cold he had experienced on the trail. The wind still howled like a pack of hungry wolves around the stone corners of the jailhouse, and Torn was immensely grateful just to be inside. He didn't much like being locked up; ever since his sixteen months as a prisoner of war at Point Lookout he'd had a strong aversion to being confined against his will. But under the circumstances, he was glad to be here rather than out in that blizzard.

"What are you doing?" queried Havelock.

"I'm going to get some sleep, if you'll quit asking me questions."

"Sleep? How can you sleep after what that son of a bitch just told us?"

"Worry about tomorrow when it comes," advised Torn, yawning.

He rolled over on his side and drifted off into a dream-shattered sleep.

CHAPTER 22

JULY 2, 1863.

They had crossed the Potomac a little more than two weeks ago. The Army of Northern Virginia—Lee's Miserables—was invading the North. It was the second time the Confederates had taken the war to the enemy. The first time, last September, the campaign had ended at Antietam. It had not ended well. In fact, the rebels had been fortunate to escape back into Virginia. The best that could be said for Antietam was that it had been a draw. An extremely bloody draw.

Torn hoped they would fare better this go-around.

The Confederacy was hard-pressed. The Union was meeting with success in the West. Vicksburg was under siege. And if Vicksburg fell, the federals would own the Mississippi. The South would be cut in half and well on the road to final defeat.

Two months ago Lee had won his most impressive victory at Chancellorsville, defeating Fighting Joe Hooker and a bluecoat army that had outnumbered the Confederates two to one. But the triumph had been achieved at a terrible cost. Stonewall Jackson, Lee's right hand, had been slain—shot by his own men as he reconnoitered in advance of his lines.

There had been talk of detaching a division, maybe two, from the Army of Northern Virginia and transporting these troops west to reinforce the beleaguered rebels at Vicksburg. But Lee had been strongly opposed to the idea. Far better, he argued, to force the enemy to reinforce Washington with troops detached from *their* army in the West, thereby relieving the pressure on Vicksburg.

So they were marching north, a bold move, invading enemy soil, threatening the federal capital by the flank, throwing the North into panic.

Torn sat with his brother Stewart and cousin Brett Yarnell around a crackling fire in a field on the outskirts of a Pennsylvania hamlet called Hunterstown, discussing the situation.

"I have a bad feeling about this," said Stewart. "I think we've bitten off more than we can chew. I don't feel right, being this far north of the Potomac."

Torn glanced at his younger brother, now a captain in the First South Carolina Cavalry—Torn's regiment. Torn had been promoted to the rank of colonel, taking command of the First after Antietam, where his predecessor had fallen in the heavy fighting around Dunkard Church.

Stewart's face was pale and drawn with pain. He had a tight dressing, spotted with blood, on his left arm above the elbow.

The sun of July 2nd had set on a fierce cavalry clash in and around Hunterstown, between Wade Hampton's South Carolina regiments and federal sabers commanded by Kilpatrick and Custer. Stewart's company had fought troops led by the dashing Custer himself, the "Boy General," the darling of the northern press, in the fields of the Gilbert Farm just south of town. Stewart had been cut by a saber. It wasn't a life-threatening wound, nor was it the first Stewart had suffered in the war, but Torn was nonetheless concerned.

He found it remarkable that, of the three of them, only Brett had been seriously wounded after so many hard-fought campaigns. Brett's right arm had been shattered by a cannonball and amputated at the elbow. Though he had lost part of an arm, Yarnell had as much fighting spirit as ever, and as much blind faith in ultimate victory as he'd always had.

"Everything this army bites off," said Brett, "it chews up and spits out. Ask McClellan and Pope and Burnside and Hooker. We sure chewed up their armies."

"Victory is habit-forming," said Torn. "We've always beaten them, and I believe we will this time."

"Not always," argued Stewart. "We didn't beat them at Antietam. Had they been better led that day they would have destroyed us. We were lucky. McClellan was a fool to attack our lines piecemeal that way. You know it's so, Clay. Now they have better leaders, and they fight better. Believe that, if nothing else. We saw abundant evidence today."

"That's because we crossed swords with Custer today," said Brett. "The man fights like a Southerner." He shook his head, smiling ruefully. "You know, Colonel, we almost got him this time."

"'Almost' doesn't count," said Stewart, "except in horseshoes."

"Custer's horse was shot out from under him," Brett told Torn. "I saw it, plain as day. One of our boys, Harbaugh, rode right up to him and aimed his carbine at Custer's head."

"But it was Harbaugh who ended up dead," said Stewart glumly. "Along with twenty others in the company. And Custer got away."

"Must be Irish, with his luck," groused Brett. "One day his luck will run out."

Stewart fed another log into the fire, searched the darkness that encompassed them. The regiment was camped in a field surrounded by black, brooding woods.

The men of the First were gathered around dozens of fires. There was no laughing, no loud talk. Torn could not fail to notice how subdued was their mood. Two years of campaigning had tempered their enthusiasm. Most of them were veterans, and war no longer seemed a lark. Grim resolve had replaced the exuberance they had displayed in the glorious early days of the war.

The tenor of the war had changed, mused Torn. It was a hard and bitter struggle for survival now.

Even a year ago things had not seemed so deadly and desperate.

"I think," Stewart said slowly, "that we left our luck on the other side of the Potomac."

"I don't follow," said Torn.

"Look, Clay. You say we've always won, and we always have when we're south of the Potomac, defending Confederate soil against Yankee invaders. We win because we're in the right. But this isn't right. We're the invaders now. Up here the Yankees are defending *their* soil, and that makes a man fight harder."

"I like the idea of coming up here," said Yarnell, contentious as always. "By God, we've fought on every inch of Virginia ground. The Old Dominion's been laid to waste. I say let the Yankees find out what it's like to have a war waged on their doorstep for a change."

"In a way, you're both right," said Torn. "This is a gamble, but one we must take. The federals grow stronger while we become weaker. They have more men, more guns."

"All the more reason to fight a defensive war," said Stewart.

"But who knows how many more invasions we can withstand? How many more times can we turn the enemy away from Richmond? We've got to buy some time. Time is our best ally. The Northern people are growing tired of war. Next year, the presidential election. If the Democrats can beat Lincoln, they'll talk peace. All we have to do is hold on. Lincoln can't win unless his army beats us. If we can keep the federals busy up here, they won't have a chance to strike at Richmond this year."

"If we win up here, it might work," Stewart said skeptically.

"*If* we win!" cried Yarnell, incredulous.

Cannon boomed in the distance.

All day long they had heard the sounds of a major battle miles to the south, near a town called Gettysburg. In that direction Stuart's cavalry had been riding; the battle at Hunterstown had delayed Hampton's command, but Torn believed they would reach the battleground by early tomorrow.

Reports indicated the opposing armies had been engaged in fierce fighting for two days. It was rumored that Lee was angry with Stuart, who had led his cavalry in what some considered a frivolous excursion completely around the federals—an exploit reminiscent of his extraordinary achievement last year, circling McClellan during the Peninsula Campaign.

Stuart's assignment had been twofold: to screen the invasion of the Army of Northern Virginia through the mountains to the west from the federals concentrated around Washington to the east, and to keep Lee informed of enemy movements.

But Stuart had lost contact with Lee's army and had remained out of touch for an entire week, leaving Lee for all intents and purposes groping blindly northward through unknown territory. To compound the problem, the federal Army of the Potomac, now under the command of George Meade, had moved in pursuit of Lee with uncharacteristic dispatch, and the

Gray Fox had stumbled upon them, in strong defensive positions in the hills around Gettysburg. For once, Lee was going to have to fight on ground not of his own choosing.

Now Stuart and his cavalry were racing to the sound of the guns. Torn was not alone in hoping the corps would not be too late for what would surely be the most crucial battle of the war.

The cannon fell silent. Torn expected to hear only sporadic gunfire during the night. Fighting in earnest would resume with the rising of the sun.

Stewart and Brett tried to get some sleep, rolling up in their blankets on the ground. Torn took a small writing case from his panniers and penned a letter to Melony Hancock. He had not seen his fiancée for nine months. It had been that long since his last furlough. He missed her. Wondered, as he did before every battle, whether he would live to see her, hold her, again.

His words were optimistic. He was confident, he wrote, that in the coming days the fate of the Confederacy would be determined, the war would soon be over, victory would be theirs, and he would return to her for good. He assured her she was always in his thoughts and reminded her that their separation was a sacrifice borne for a just cause. They fought for the same fundamental rights their forefathers had fought and died for in the American Revolution, the most basic of which was the right to be free of a government that did not respect their way of life. This was a right firmly grounded in the foremost tenet of democracy: that a government derived its power solely from the consent of the governed. . . .

He sat staring into the dying fire, pen poised over paper, for a very long time. He realized he was not nearly as optimistic as the letter indicated. Stewart's grave doubts had had an effect on him. He had a presentiment of disaster.

A log settled in the fire, sending a shower of orange sparks skyward and rousing him from grim reverie. He signed the letter, folded it neatly, and put it in a pocket of his gray tunic. He hoped that, if he died tomorrow, someone would find the letter and see it delivered.

He had no way of knowing that something much worse than death lay in store for him.

23

JULY 3, 1863. MORNING.

The previous day's fighting around Gettysburg had left eight thousand dead and wounded strewn between lines that, for all the blood and sacrifice, were little changed from the day before. Poor communication and a position that stretched five miles in length had rendered Lee's assaults on the entrenched federals largely ineffectual.

On the right, Longstreet had tried without success to dislodge the bluecoats from the Round Tops and Devil's Den. Some regiments in his corps reported losses in excess of eighty percent.

In the center, A. P. Hill, the fiery corps commander who wore a red battle shirt into combat, had failed to budge the enemy dug in along Cemetery Ridge.

Only as the second day of battle drew to a close had Ewell on the rebel left managed to coordinate a costly and futile assault on Culp's Hill, a bloody struggle halted by darkness.

Stuart's Cavalry Corps arrived on the battlefield shortly after daybreak. The men were ordered to draw ammunition from waiting ordnance wagons. Stung by Lee's cold reproach the night before, Stuart dispatched Torn to army headquarters.

"Advise General Lee we will be ready to engage the enemy in two hours," Stuart told Torn, "and confirm that the orders he gave me last night have not changed."

Torn knew he had been chosen for the task at random, but he was honored nonetheless and looked forward to seeing Robert E. Lee in person. All of Stuart's staff were busy with affairs within the corps, and he was the first officer Stuart had happened across whose rank was appropriate for contact with the supreme commander of the Army of Northern Virginia.

As he rode west from town in the direction of Seminary Ridge and the center of the Confederate line, the air was cool and damp on his face. White mist clung to low-lying areas and rose slowly through the trees to blot out the brightening sky. Dew dripped from the leaves, making a sound like rain in the woods.

He found Lee and Longstreet and their staffs on the eastern slope of Seminary Ridge, in front of the Confederate position. Behind the ridge, and screened from the view of the enemy by the wooded heights, a great deal of troop movement could be heard.

To his right—eastward—Torn could look out across a valley carpeted by the cottony morning mist. This bottomland, with Seminary Ridge on the west and Cemetery Ridge to the east, was largely open, cultivated ground, fourteen hundred yards wide. He could still see the flickering of the federals' morning cook fires all along Cemetery Ridge, and when he paused to scan the ridge with his field glasses, he could tell it was fairly bristling with cannon. Seldom had he seen such a strong position, and he thought it looked much like the Confederate fortifications along Marye's Heights, which the federals had tried so disastrously to storm in the Battle of Fredericksburg a year earlier.

Like everyone else in the Army of Northern Virginia, Torn revered Robert E. Lee; he stood in awe of the man he wholeheartedly believed to be one of the greatest soldiers in history. His faith in Lee's ability to lead them to ultimate triumph was complete and unshakable.

The beloved general was in his fifty-seventh year, white-bearded and red-faced. He looked fit and serene, and Torn was blissfully unaware—as was almost everyone else—that Lee had lately been suffering from the heart disease that would eventually take his life. Lee wore an old gray coat and a gray hat without insignia.

He was a man of iron will and complete self-control. A temperate, God-fearing man who did not smoke or drink or gamble or swear. He was the paragon of Southern chivalry. This morning he rode his white charger, Traveler, and as Torn approached and saluted smartly, Lee was sitting erect in the saddle, gauntlet-covered hands resting lightly on the pommel, gazing intently across the valley at the center of the Army of the Potomac.

"Good morning, Colonel," said Lee. "What news do you have for me this morning?"

"General Stuart sends his compliments and wishes me to inform you he will be ready to move upon the enemy by ten o'clock."

Lee nodded. "Good, good. I am relieved to have my cavalry on hand. I feel better knowing Jeb Stuart will be with us on this momentous day."

"The general also wishes to confirm the orders you gave him last night concerning the deployment of the corps."

Lee glanced at a large full-bearded man sitting his horse alongside. This was James Longstreet, "Old Pete" to his friends, and the man Lee fondly called his "old war-horse."

Longstreet's eyes were a cold and piercing blue, his beard cinnamon-colored. He was a brusque, slow-talking, stubborn man, a proven leader and a keen strategist. Since Stonewall Jackson's death, he had been Lee's right hand. But he was not at all a mirror image of Jackson. Though a hard and tenacious fighter, he was much more cautious than Stonewall and rather less daring. Longstreet had produced a theory of defensive warfare, proof of his prudent nature. It was a theory that could not marshal the support of many of this particular army's cavalier-officers. As one brigadier general had said, the Army of Northern Virginia was just not cut out to wage defensive war.

"The situation is unchanged," replied Lee. "General Pickett arrived last night with a fresh division. He is aching for action. His men missed Chancellorsville, and Fredericksburg as well." Lee permitted himself a small, almost wistful smile. "He's beginning to think we've hatched some conspiracy to get through this terrible war without giving him a chance for glory. Well, he shall have his chance today. Pickett will advance and take that ridge by storm, supported by the rest of General Longstreet's corps on both flanks."

"What's left of it," mumbled Longstreet.

Lee ignored the comment. "General Hill will be in reserve. The assault will be preceded by a concentrated artillery barrage upon the enemy's trenches along Cemetery Ridge, a *pont de feu,* if you will. I want the Cavalry Corps in position on the extreme left flank of General Ewell, along the York Turnpike. God willing, Pickett's division will crack the center of the enemy, forcing him to retire. General Stuart will strike south and cut off his retreat."

"General Lee," said Longstreet, "it is my opinion that a frontal assault will be repulsed with great loss of life."

Lee's features betrayed no emotion, but his eyes were cold black orbs.

"Our scouts report Meade's entire force is now in place," continued Longstreet, plunging doggedly ahead. "We no longer enjoy a numerical advantage."

"We seldom have," said Lee.

"The roads south are open. I say flank the enemy. He will have to abandon this position in order to defend Washington, or he will turn and give battle, and this time it will be on our terms, on ground of our own choosing, and with Virginia at our backs if fortune frowns."

Lee raised an arm to point across the mist-shrouded valley at Cemetery Ridge.

"General," he said, polite but aloof, "the enemy is there, and there I will strike him."

Longstreet's stubborn streak was renowned. He was one of a handful of men not so awestruck by Lee that he would fail to speak his mind.

"This is not a good position," he said bluntly. "Meade is firmly entrenched. He has a great many cannon on that ridge, and the crews manning those cannon know their business, as these last two days have amply illustrated. His artillery commands completely the open ground our assault must cross. Worse, his lines form a half circle, and anywhere we strike he is able to bring up quick reinforcements."

"Pickett's men can do it," said Lee. "They are fifteen thousand strong, and they will sweep the federals from that ridge."

It seemed to Torn that if this man willed it, it would be so.

"I have been a soldier all my life, General," said Longstreet, with quiet despair. "I believe I know as well as anyone what soldiers can do. Never have there been soldiers such as these we command in this army. Never in history has there been such an army. It has accomplished what no other army its size has ever accomplished. But it is my opinion that there never were fifteen thousand men who could advance fourteen hundred yards over open ground under the artillery present on that ridge and, I might add, under enfilading fire by more artillery from Round Top."

"Pickett's men will break the enemy's center," said Lee, very softly, and looked away.

Longstreet said no more. Having stated his case, he would carry out his orders to the best of his ability, which was considerable, and regardless of whether he agreed with those orders.

Lee motioned to one of his aides, who produced a map of Gettysburg and the surrounding area. Using this map, Lee showed Torn the deployment of the Cavalry Corps as he desired it. With this information, Torn took his leave.

He rode north off the ridge and struck the Hagerstown Road, where he turned east toward Gettysburg. Cannon roared from somewhere up ahead, on the other side of town, a fierce artillery duel, which Torn surmised was being waged around Culp's Hill.

The sun was beginning to burn the mist apart, and the heat began to build. Out in the fields lay uncounted dead, bloated corpses of men and horses. Ambulances and burial details moved through the war's gory debris. Torn rode past a peach orchard where every single leaf had been stripped from the branches by a hail of musket balls.

Doubt gnawed at the edges of his confidence. Now

he knew his brother was not alone in his opinion that this situation boded ill for the army. Longstreet was apparently of like mind.

Rationally, Torn couldn't believe that fifteen thousand men could cross so much open ground under so many guns and emerge victorious. But this army, as Old Pete had said, was special. One of a kind. It had done extraordinary things before. And Lee had earned the trust and faith of every soldier. If Lee said it could be done . . .

He rode on, to a place that would come to be called East Cavalry Field—a place where his life would be changed forever.

CHAPTER

24

THE CAVALRY CORPS RODE EAST OUT OF GET-
tysburg. Scouts brought word that Gregg's Yankee
cavalry division was guarding Meade's right wing and
was concentrated along the Low Dutch Road, near
its intersection with the Hanover Road. This was a
major crossroad. Stuart knew that if he could seize
and hold it, his cavalry would stand directly across
the path the enemy would take in retreat. If Pickett's
attack succeeded, Stuart could in effect slam the back
door shut, and the withdrawal of the Army of the
Potomac would become a certifiable rout.

They rode several miles on the York Turnpike,
through rich farmland. Heat shimmered in the fields.
At noon began the most tremendous artillery barrage
Torn had ever heard. These were Porter Alex-
ander's 160 guns, pounding the federal position along

Cemetery Ridge, the precursor to the frontal assault by Pickett's division. The bombardment lasted for over an hour.

Stuart turned off the turnpike and took his command to the rim of the densely wooded Cress Ridge. There seven thousand rebel horse soldiers paused while Stuart called his regimental and brigade commanders to a brief council. He succinctly explained what he hoped to accomplish.

"Gentlemen, our purpose is twofold. First, we must protect General Ewell's left flank. Second, we are to strike the enemy behind his lines should the opportunity present itself."

He pointed to the valley south of the ridge. It was farmland for the most part, fields separated by stone and rail fences, some hedgerows, isolated groves of trees.

"As you can see," continued Stuart, "we can observe every road leading from the rear of the federal army. The ground is open, conducive to cavalry operations. In fact, I daresay not even Murat at the Battle of Jena had such splendid terrain for a mounted charge. When the time comes, we will attack by columns of squadron, with General Hampton's brigade to the right of General Fitz Lee's brigade. General Chambliss's brigade will hold this ridge. You will wait for my signal. May God ride with us, for on this day we may secure the future of the Confederacy."

Returning to the First South Carolina, Torn called his squadron commanders together and told them what to expect.

"Murat at Jena!" exclaimed Stewart, after Torn

had repeated the general's orders. "More like the Light Brigade at Balaklava, if you ask me. Into the valley of death."

Torn grimaced. The assault by British cavalry to which his brother referred had been heroic but ill-advised, with disastrous consequences, part of one of the major battles in the recent Crimean War. Stewart's comparison, in Torn's opinion, was just as ill-advised.

"Since Captain Torn has misgivings," Hadley Fourcade said with thinly disguised derision, "may I request that the colonel allow my squadron to lead the First South Carolina."

Torn bit back a sharp retort. Essentially Hadley was calling his brother a coward. Under the circumstances, though, Torn did not feel it proper to leap to Stewart's defense. He could not permit personal considerations to cloud his judgment or impair his ability to command. He did not doubt Stewart's courage or his commitment to the Cause, but he was growing more than a little tired of his brother's pessimism.

"You may have the lead, Captain Fourcade," he said.

All the officers but Stewart returned to their commands.

"I assume," Stewart said stiffly, "that you will be at the head of the regiment."

"Of course."

"Which will put Hadley at your back. I believe that to be a grave mistake, Clay, for reasons that should be obvious."

"I've made my decision."

"Don't you see what General Stuart is doing? He's going to try his damnedest to make amends for failing General Lee. A straight-on charge à la Murat has never succeeded in this war. It is an outdated tactic."

"We will obey orders," Torn snapped. "If you are of another mind, you may be relieved of your command."

"'Theirs not to reason why,'" Stewart snapped. Stung by Torn's reprimand, he spun on his heel and walked away.

From his vantage point on the ridge, Torn scanned the valley below with field glasses. He saw Union cavalry—Gregg's division—in the fields near the intersection of the Low Dutch and Hanover roads, a mile due south. To the west, where the balance of the opposing armies confronted one another, the continuous thunder of artillery fire rolled across the Pennsylvania countryside. A pall of powder smoke hung above the heights around Gettysburg.

Within the hour, Yankee skirmishers had ventured closer to Cress Ridge and were engaging Confederate advance units around a barn and outbuildings three hundred yards south of where Torn stood. A rebel battery—Griffin's—opened fire from the foot of the ridge, pummeling the advancing bluecoats. Confederate sharpshooters laid down a highly effective fire from the barn and adjacent fence lines.

The rattle of musket fire was punctuated by the bark of cannon. A federal battery joined the action. The Yankee gun crews were excellent and destroyed two of the rebel guns in as many minutes, forcing Griffin to retire.

Dismounted troopers, blue and gray, were thrown into the fray around the barn, and what had begun as a skirmish quickly escalated into a fiercely fought engagement. Torn thought it was fast approaching the perfect time for a mounted charge, with so many of the enemy units afoot, and even as this occurred to him he saw the First Virginia emerge from the woods to his right at a spirited gallop, sabers flashing in the sunlight, gray riders rending the air with their yells.

A federal regiment rode forward to meet this charge. Its battle flag identified the unit as the Seventh Michigan. Torn looked for and located George Custer, as usual leading his Wolverines, well out in front of his men, spurning danger and riding like a demon, his yellow hair streaming.

The opposing cavalry met with a crash at a stone and rail fence, exchanging carbine and pistol fire at point-blank range. A cloud of smoke obscured the melee. Torn held his breath until he saw the Michigan troopers streaming south in a disorderly withdrawal. Custer, mused Torn, attacked splendidly, but did not retreat very well. The Virginians regrouped and pressed on, only to be met and stopped by the murderous canister fire of a Yankee battery. Bloodily repulsed, the First Virginia drifted back toward Cress Ridge.

Torn was chafing at the bit. He did not like the role of spectator. He was contemplating the wisdom of riding to Stuart and urging a full-scale assault when one of Wade Hampton's aides arrived. The brigade staff member snapped off a brisk salute.

"General Hampton is highly pleased to afford the First South Carolina the privilege of leading the column, sir."

"Good!" Torn said sharply. "Good!"

He leaped for his charger. The regimental color guard and bugler drew near. Torn swept the valley below with glittering steel-cast eyes.

"Beg pardon, Colonel?"

Torn looked over his shoulder. It was the sergeant of the color guard who had queried, leaning forward in his saddle, a puzzled look on his face. Torn realized he'd been mumbling aloud.

"Lord Tennyson, Sergeant," he replied, embarrassed.

This information failed to edify the sergeant, who nodded, still puzzled but pretending to understand.

Torn credited Stewart, who had quoted the poet a while ago, for bringing the immortal words to mind.

> Cannon to right of them,
> Cannon to left of them,
> Cannon in front of them
> Volleyed and thundered.
> Into the jaws of death,
> Into the mouth of hell
> Rode the six hundred.

He drew his saber and led the First South Carolina down the southern slope of the ridge, out of the woods, and into the valley.

CHAPTER 25

THE FIRST SOUTH CAROLINA ADVANCED IN COL-
umn by squadron, followed by the other regiments
in Hampton's brigade. To their left rode Fitz Lee's
brigade, Virginians for the most part. The summer
sun reflected off thousands of sabers. It was an awe-
some martial display, almost three thousand
mounted fighters in attack formation—a sight that
had rarely been seen in this war. The two brigades
represented the cream of the Confederate cavalry.
Many of the rebel horsemen expected the federals
to turn tail and run. The Yankees had done so before.
Union cavalry, in general, had been no match for
them.

Today proved to be different.

Surrounded by a swarm of aides and a color guard
bearing his personal battle flag, Wade Hampton gal-

loped to the head of the column. Hampton was a
bearded giant, of grand physique and manner. A
gentleman of the first order, he was South Carolina's
favorite son. Prior to the outbreak of hostilities, he
had been a prosperous planter. Out of his own pocket
he had financed the Hampton Legion, the first vol-
unteers from the Palmetto State. Though not a
professional soldier, he had proven himself worthy
of his rank and of the esteem in which he was held
by his men. Among the dashing *beaux sabreurs* of
the Confederate cavalry, he was honored second
only to J. E. B. Stuart. It came as no surprise to
Torn that South Carolina's *grand seigneur* was going
to lead the charge.

The two brigade columns maintained perfect align-
ment as their gait increased from trot to gallop. Yankee skirmishers fired at them from behind fence lines
and hedgerows. The rebel onslaught swept over
them. The thunder of thousands of horses at a dead
run made the earth shudder.

Federal cannon fired double canister, tearing
bloody holes in the gray ranks. Horses somersaulted,
flinging dead or dying men through the air. The Confederates rode dauntlessly on, seemingly unstop-
pable.

As they closed on the federal batteries, the Yankee
guns were pulled back. A Union regiment, the First
Michigan, rushed forward to meet the rebel attack
head on. Torn saw a lithe figure on a black charger
four lengths in front of the Michigan horse soldiers.
The man was swinging his saber overhead. Long
yellow hair streamed out beneath his campaign hat.

It was George Armstrong Custer, exhorting his men.

"Come on, you Wolverines!"

The First Michigan plowed headlong into the First South Carolina.

Sabers clashed, pistols barked, men yelled and cursed and screamed in pain—the deafening din of battle.

Though the five hundred Wolverines were sorely outnumbered, their bold counterattack drove a wedge into the Hampton brigade, halting it. More Union squadrons poured in from all sides, and still more engaged Fitz Lee's Virginians.

In this mad melee, Torn fought with cold fury, felling several Yankee troopers. Directly ahead of him, federals swarmed Hampton's coterie. Hampton himself took several saber blows to the head. Blinded by his own blood, he clung stubbornly to his saddle and continued to fight until one of his aides—more concerned for Hampton's life than Hampton was himself—led the general back to Cress Ridge.

Hampton's standard-bearer was the focus of ferocious enemy attention. Every Yankee cavalryman wanted the honor of capturing such a famous battle flag. The standard-bearer was shot off his horse. Torn spurred his own mount forward, virtually decapitating a Union trooper who had jumped to the ground with the intention of recovering Hampton's gold-fringed colors. As the man toppled in a spray of blood, Torn snatched the flag out of his dying grasp.

His charger rearing, Torn raised the standard high.

"South Carolina to me!"

A ragged cheer mingled with shrill fox hunter yells rose above the clamor of battle. The First South Carolina seemed to surge forward as one, driving the hard-fighting Wolverines before them. Brett Yarnell brawled his way to Torn's side. Grinning, he grabbed the flagstaff.

"If you'll give me the honor, Colonel."

Torn relinquished the battle flag.

At that moment, just as the Confederates seemed on the verge of overwhelming the First Michigan, a squadron of the Third Pennsylvania arrived on their flank and fired their carbines into the gray riders, a murderous volley. Dozens of rebel soldiers fell. A bullet snapped the flagstaff in two. The standard fluttered to the ground. A hail of hot lead tore into Brett Yarnell. He swayed in the saddle, then slid to the ground. Torn was struck in the thigh, a numbing blow. The Confederates recoiled. The column disintegrated. The remnants began to fall back. The Pennsylvanians kept up the withering rifle fire. Custer rallied his Wolverines. They rushed forward with renewed vigor, slamming into the stunned rebels.

Sick at heart, Torn looked down at Yarnell. His cousin's tunic was soaked with blood. His dead eyes stared at the sky. Brett was still grinning and still clutching the sundered flagstaff.

"Clay!"

It was Stewart, struggling against the tide of retreat to reach his brother's side.

"Clay, we must withdraw!"

Torn nodded grimly, dug spur.

The federals gave hot pursuit. Torn caught up with his men, rallied them near a stone and rail fence. He ordered what was left of the regiment to dismount and form behind the fence. They halted the Michigan troopers with a devastating fusillade of pistol and carbine fire. A ragged cheer swelled from the parched throats of the South Carolina boys.

Torn limped along the line, encouraging his men. He threw a quick look around. The remnants of the two Confederate columns were melting into the trees on Cress Ridge. On all sides severe fighting marked pockets of rebel resistance on the field of battle. Rebel artillery tried to assist, sending cannonballs screaming overhead to punish the oncoming Yankees.

The Wolverines in front of Torn drew back, regrouped. A squadron detached itself and swung to the west. Torn knew they meant to outflank him. He found Hadley Fourcade on the right wing of the thin gray line, alerted him to the flanking movement.

Another fence joined the line they now held at a wide oblique angle. Torn ordered Hadley to take his squadron there and turn back the Yankees.

"You must hold the line, Captain," said Torn. "If you fail, we'll be cut off."

"I'll hold it," snapped Hadley, as though he resented Torn for even speculating about what might happen if he did not.

As Fourcade realigned his squadron on the right

flank, Torn turned back to the center of the South Carolina position and was met by his brother.

"Perhaps we should withdraw," Stewart suggested.

Torn scanned the field again. The federals were gathering themselves for another charge. Cress Ridge was three hundred yards to the rear.

"We'll turn them back once more," Torn decided. "Then we'll withdraw. We must give the rest of the brigade time to regroup on the ridge."

"You've been wounded."

Torn felt the blood streaming down his leg, filling his boot. He knew it was a serious wound, but the pain was tolerable—an enormous ache spreading throughout his body. He wondered if he would lose the leg. For him, one of the most ghastly sights of the war had been the stacks of amputated limbs all too often seen outside field hospitals. He could imagine, vividly, a surgeon taking a saw to his leg. Then he reminded himself that he could very possibly lose more than a leg in the next few minutes.

"Hold the left flank, Stewart."

Stewart started to turn away, swung back around, and held out his hand.

"Good luck, brother."

Torn grasped the hand firmly. He was far more concerned for Stewart than he was for himself.

The First Michigan charged.

Saber in one hand, pistol in the other, Torn stalked back and forth along the center of the line.

"Pick your targets, men. We've never been

whipped before. The Corps is watching. Show them what you're made of."

Howling, the Wolverines bore down on them, saber steel gleaming like molten silver in the hot sunlight, pistols spitting flame and white powder smoke.

And then a squadron of bluecoats fell on them from the rear, scattering their horses held in reserve, decimating the ranks of the First South Carolina with an appalling fire.

Caught in a frightful crossfire, Torn's regiment abandoned the fence line. It was every man for himself now. Torn caught a glimpse of Hadley's squadron fleeing toward the trees. Instinctively he headed for Stewart's position. A Yankee trooper blocked his path, fired a pistol at Torn's head, but his rearing horse spoiled his aim. Torn shot him out of the saddle. The riderless horse galloped away. Through eye-burning swirls of gun smoke, Torn spotted his brother.

"Stewart!"

Stewart turned, took a step, staggered as bullets struck him in the side. Reeling, he fought to keep his feet, stared with astonishment at Torn. Another bullet hit him in the neck, and he went down.

He was dead before Torn reached him.

Stunned, Torn dropped his weapons and fell to his knees beside his brother's body. The tumult of battle quickly subsided, but he didn't know it. He heard nothing. Felt nothing. He held Stewart in his arms and only gradually became aware of several mounted bluecoats surrounding him.

He looked up into the icy blue eyes of George Armstrong Custer.

Custer gave him a curt but civil nod. "Colonel." The Boy General glanced at Stewart, and compassion softened the taut lines of his angular face. "Family?"

"Yes."

"My deepest condolences," Custer said sincerely. He turned to the soldier next to him. "Sergeant, take charge of the prisoner."

CHAPTER 26

"BAD DREAMS?" ASKED HADLEY, TAUNTING HIM.

Torn sat up in the bunk. He looked around to get his bearings. Havelock and Armstrong, it seemed, had taken his advice; they were sleeping soundly in the adjacent cell, the marshal sawing logs on the bunk, the young deputy lying on the floor wrapped in the blanket.

Hadley stood just outside Torn's cell. The guard was sitting in a ladder-back chair at the other end of the cellblock, smoking a quirly. It was still dark outside, but the wind had stopped howling.

"What do you want?" asked Torn.

"Thought we'd talk over old times. This will be our last chance."

"We've got nothing to talk about."

"Yes, we do. Let's talk about Branson's sister. How did she get shot?"

"Like I said. One of your outlaws did it, Hadley."

Fourcade curtly shook his head. "Not outlaws. Partisan rangers. Guerrillas, if you must. Not outlaws."

"'A rose by any other name.'"

"Must have been the five I sent back along the Pacific tracks. We were headed here, after taking care of business at the train. Cut the sign of two riders going east. Sent those five to find out who those riders were. I suppose you must have been one of them. Who was the other? And where is he?"

"'Taking care of business'?" Torn's short laugh was derisive. "Is that what you call it? I call it cold-blooded murder."

"You don't want to tell me about the other man? Fine. It doesn't matter. But what happened to my five men?"

"They're dead."

Hadley hiked an eyebrow. "You've done some damage, Clay."

"Glad to hear it."

"It was right foolish, you and these lawmen coming into Cass County like this with Branson. But then, strategy was never your strong suit. The regiment should have been mine, for that reason alone. I believe recent events prove that to be true. I've outfoxed you at every turn. Admit it."

Torn rose, went to the strap-iron wall separating them.

"You know, Hadley, looking back, it strikes me

that our quarrel got the better of us. It didn't have to be this way, but what's done is done. It's past time we settled this."

"You're going to hang tomorrow, Clay, so I'd say it's settled. What did you expect? A fair fight? Pistols at twenty paces?" Hadley snorted. "If our positions were reversed—if I were in there, and you were out here—you'd hang me without blinking an eye, wouldn't you, Judge?"

"No, I'd settle it man to man."

"You're just blowing smoke."

"You're a coward, Hadley."

Hadley lashed out, grabbed the strap iron. Torn didn't blink an eye.

"You called me that once before, in Talleysville. Remember? I should have killed you then."

"You tried."

"This time I'll do better than try. Like I said, you're a traitor to the Confederacy. Traitors deserve to hang."

Torn smirked. "Still a soldier gallantly fighting a war, is that it? How do you justify murdering three defenseless men today?"

"We tried to fight the Yankees honorably. But they don't know anything about honor. The South seceded peaceably. All we wanted was freedom from the oppression of abolitionist tyrants. It was a right guaranteed us by the Constitution. But the Yankees care as little about the law as they do about honor. They invaded our land, burned our homes, violated our women. They said they were trying to preserve the Union. A bloody lie, and we both know it. They wanted to destroy our economy, our way of life, because the South had become too strong. They said they wanted to free the slaves, but they treat them worse than we ever did. They never gave a damn about the well-being of the slaves. But they knew they could ruin us if they took our labor force away, and that's the real reason behind emancipation."

"You've used that excuse so long, I think you actually believe it."

"My men and I will never surrender," vowed Hadley. "Ours is a noble cause. We've driven the Yankees out of Cass County. As long as one of us lives, the Confederacy lives. You think I don't know what your scheme was? You thought you could turn the people against me. Can't be done. The people know I fight for them. I destroy the destroyers. Exploit the exploiters. I prey on the Yankee-run institutions that in turn try to prey on the people."

"The banks and the railroads."

"Exactly."

"Cass County's very own Robin Hood. But what about the money you steal? Do you give it to the poor, Hadley? Or do you line your own pockets?"

Hadley's features darkened.

"I wouldn't expect you to understand," he said bitterly. "But the people know. As do their representatives in the state legislature, I might add." With relish, Hadley produced a folded newspaper page from a coat pocket, presented it to Torn. "You'll notice a front-page article concerning an amnesty bill. Read the quote from the bill itself."

He fetched a lantern off a nail in the wall, held it

high to throw its light onto the newspaper page in Torn's hands.

Torn read: "'Whereas these men, who imperil their lives in defense of their principles, are made desperate, driven as they are from the fields of honest industry, from their families and friends, their honor and their country, they can know no law but the law of self-preservation, and their lot is not of their choosing. They are not outlaws, but rather brave men whose vigilance has protected hundreds of homes and thousands of lives from desecration. . . . '"

Torn folded the paper, passed it through a gap in the strap iron, shaking his head. "That bill didn't come close to passing."

"One day it will."

"Not a chance."

"They've even written a song about me. How do you like that, Clay? A song, by God: 'Come all you bold robbers and open your ears. Of Hadley Fourcade you quickly will hear. With his band of bold riders in double-quick time, he rides to Cass County to hold the line.'"

"You think right highly of yourself," said Torn. "That part about holding the line, though. Whoever wrote that ballad didn't know about Gettysburg, did he? He didn't know about the line you failed to hold at East Cavalry Field that day."

Hadley's eyes burned with hate. "I've got a little secret to share with you, Clay. I could have held that position. But I didn't. You know why? Because I wanted what was rightfully mine. The regiment.

But most of all, I wanted to see you dead."

Pleased by the expression on Torn's face, he spun on his heel and started to walk away.

"Hadley."

It was soft-spoken, scarcely more than a whisper. Fourcade paused, looked back.

"My brother died that day," said Torn. "I blame you for his death. This doesn't have anything to do with the law anymore. This is personal."

"It always has been," replied Hadley, and left the cellblock.

CHAPTER

27

TORN SPENT THE REST OF THE NIGHT SITTING ON
the edge of the bunk and staring at the floor.

Hadley's revelation had not come as a complete
shock to him. He'd wondered every day since the
battle at East Cavalry Field whether Fourcade had
abandoned his position on the First South Carolina's
right flank out of spite or for defensible military reasons.

Suspicions aside, Torn had always before con-
cluded that, no matter how much Hadley hated him,
Fourcade wouldn't have sacrificed so many lives for
the sake of some personal vendetta. Not even Hadley
would stoop so low. Torn had tried to convince himself that the federals had broken through the right
flank, throwing Fourcade's squadron into retreat.

Now he knew the truth.

Stewart had been right all along. Poor Stewart. Torn blamed himself for his brother's death as much as he blamed Hadley. Maybe more. If he'd only listened to Stewart . . . If only he'd killed Hadley when he had the chance, that night on the road out of Talleysville. Then perhaps the right flank would have held. Perhaps they would have made an orderly withdrawal back to Cress Ridge. Perhaps Stewart would still be alive.

He could carry this speculation even further. If he hadn't been captured, he might possibly have returned to South Carolina in time to prevent, somehow, Melony Hancock's abduction by Yankee deserters. The Southern cause had been lost at Gettysburg—that much was certain. But he and Melony might have been able to rebuild their lives after the war's end.

Torn realized this kind of conjecture was bootless. Worse, it was pure agony. But he couldn't help thinking that Hadley Fourcade was responsible for a lot of the calamity that had befallen him since that fateful day at East Cavalry Field. And it was not Torn's way to forgive and forget. If he got any kind of chance at all, he was going to make Hadley pay.

But what kind of chance would he get? Prospects were bleak, to say the least. He and Havelock and Armstrong were going to be hanged in the morning.

Torn grimly made up his mind to die fighting. If nothing else, he would make his play the moment they opened the cell door. They'd shoot him down, of course, but that was preferable to dancing at the end of a rope.

Dawn was slow in coming. The blizzard had blown itself out, and the morning was as still as the grave. Downstairs the bushwhackers began to stir. Torn heard gruff voices, coughing, the rattle of the coffeepot on the iron stove. The cellblock guard was slumped in his chair, snoring lightly. The lantern—the one that Hadley had carried over so that Torn could read the newspaper clipping concerning the amnesty bill—now sat on the floor just outside Torn's cell.

The lantern.

Torn stared at it, astonished by the thought flashing across his mind. Could it work? Surely not. But there was only one way to find out.

He moved to the cell door, catfooted, keeping a wary eye on the guard. Kneeling, he reached through the strap iron. He could just barely hook his fingers around the lantern's bail. Lifting the lantern, he brought it closer, set it down very gently right next to the door. Slipping his other arm through the strap iron, he grasped the bail firmly on one side of the lantern and pulled at it on the other. The bail was a curved piece of thin round iron bent at either end to pass through eyelets on a brass clamp. He had to exert a lot of force to bend the end of the bail enough to slide it out of the eyelet. The base of the lantern scraped against the floor. Torn fired a glance at the guard. The man hadn't moved, but he was no longer snoring. Torn held his breath and pulled even harder. The bail slipped out of the eyelet, and then it was an easy matter to unhook the other end.

After insinuating the curved piece of iron into the

cell through the straps on the door, Torn bent the bail relatively straight. Then he stood up and reached back out through the door, got both hands on the bail, and eased one end into the keyhole. He couldn't see the lock, had to rely on his sense of touch, so he kept his eyes glued to the guard while focusing all of his attention on attacking the lock. He was no expert on lock mechanisms. All he had to go on was the fact that the lock was worked by a large skeleton key. The bail, with the end bent at a right angle, vaguely resembled such a key.

He probed the keyway gently, keeping the short end of the bail turned downward, as the teeth of the key would be. Iron scraped against iron, but not loudly enough to awaken the guard. Torn felt a horizontal bar, and then the end of the bail slipped into a notch in that bar. He tried sliding the bar one way and, when it didn't budge, the other. This time the bar moved, with a much louder screech of iron that made Torn flinch.

The guard stirred.

Frozen, Torn watched the man for a full half minute. But the bushwhacker's eyes didn't open; he did not lift his head up off his chest. Torn drew a long, calming breath, slid the bar back as far as it would go.

Praying, he pushed gently against the cell door.

The door opened. It hit the lantern, and the base of the lantern scraped across the floor. Torn cursed himself for an unadulterated fool. But the bushwhacker didn't move.

Lady Luck, thought Torn, just dance with me a little longer.

After sliding the bail out of the keyhole, he bent down to reach through the strap iron and lift the lantern, placing it farther away from the door. Then he eased the door open enough to slip through.

With a cold smile, he walked over to the sleeping guard.

Armstrong's scattergun lay across the man's lap. Both of the bushwhacker's arms were resting on it. Torn considered the pistol in the bushwhacker's holster, then opted for the knife in the man's boot. As he drew it, the guard woke. Torn rose and struck with the knife. The man opened his mouth to yell a warning. He tried to bring the shotgun to bear. Torn's free hand clamped down over the hammers even as the blade of the knife entered the man's skull just below the chin. The force of the blow clamped his jaws shut. The blade, buried to the hilt, pierced his brain, and he died instantly. Blood drooled out of his mouth. His body spasmed. Torn held him down in the chair until he was still.

Torn listened a moment with bated breath for the sounds of activity downstairs. Someone was talking, but he couldn't make out the words, and there was no alarm in the voice.

He searched the dead man's pockets, found the key to the cells. Turning to the door of the cell holding Havelock and Armstrong, he found both men awake and standing.

"Nice work," rasped Havelock.

Torn unlocked the door, handed the scattergun to

Armstrong, who broke it open to check the loads. Havelock went to the dead man, took the pistol out of the holster.

"One of us will be without an iron," he told Torn.

"Keep the pistol," replied Torn. He pulled the knife out of the dead man's throat, wiped it clean on the bushwhacker's shirt. Havelock watched closely and noted that Torn's features were impassive.

"You're a hard man, Judge," Havelock remarked with grudging respect.

"Not by choice."

"So how do we play it?" asked Armstrong, glancing at the broken window blocked off by the upended bunk. This was the window the bushwhacker—the one Jennings had killed—had tried to escape through the night before last, and it was clear that Armstrong was considering trying to escape through it himself.

Torn looked at Havelock. The marshal looked right back at him.

"What do you think?" asked Havelock.

Torn was surprised that the marshal was asking for his opinion.

"I think we'd be fools to run for it. Better to take and hold this building."

"Assuming we can take it," said Havelock, "how long do you think we can hold it? I don't know for sure how many men Hadley has with him, but I figure we're outnumbered three to one, probably more."

"Wheeler will be here this morning," said Torn. "I sent him to Warrensburg to get help. If we keep Hadley occupied here long enough for Wheeler to get back, we might be able to rid Cass County of the bushwhackers for good."

"So you're saying we hold on until reinforcements arrive," said Havelock. "That's what the men at the Alamo tried to do, as I recall. You know what happened to them."

"Look," Torn said curtly. "I'm staying. I aim to kill Hadley Fourcade. He and I have been fighting a duel for years, Marshal. It's past time we settled things."

"I say we stay and fight," voted Armstrong.

Havelock smiled. "Me, too. I'm too damned old to be climbing out of second-story windows. Probably'd break my fool neck trying."

They heard someone coming up the stairs. Two long strides carried Torn to the lantern. He extinguished the flame, plunging the cellblock into darkness. Thin gray dawn-light leaked through the windows. Torn and the lawmen crouched in the shadows until the man reached the top of the steps. Then Torn jumped him, pinned him against a wall, and pressed the blade of the knife against his throat.

Torn was a tick's hair away from cutting the man from ear to ear when he recognized Caleb Branson. He wasn't sure why he did it, but he hesitated.

"Kill him!" hissed Havelock.

"Wish you wouldn't," Branson said with admirable calm. "I've come to help."

CHAPTER 28

"If you don't kill him, Judge," growled Havelock, "I will."

The marshal thumbed back the hammer of his pistol.

"I brought your gun, Judge," said Branson. "It's in the back of my belt."

Caleb was wearing a duster. Torn kept the knife pressed to his throat while he reached around him to pull the Colt Peacemaker free.

"How did you get this?" Torn asked.

"Hadley gave it to me. He swears by his .44 Starr. Said after what I'd been through, I deserved a souvenir. He kept your knife."

"It's a trap," said Havelock.

Torn took the knife away from Branson's throat.

"Why would Hadley lay a trap for us, Marshal?"

he asked. "Far as he knows, we're locked up tight in our cells."

Havelock scowled. He didn't trust Branson, but he couldn't come up with an answer.

Branson was rubbing his throat. He glanced at the dead guard.

"I was going to take over for Riles, then let you out. But it appears you didn't need my help after all."

"How many downstairs?" asked Armstrong.

"Just three. Hadley and a couple of others left a few minutes ago to get breakfast over at the hotel."

"What were you planning to do after you broke us out?"

"Horses are in the livery," said Branson. "We ride out, taking as many of the other mounts with us as we can."

"How many men does Hadley have in all?"

Branson did some quick mental addition. "Without Riles, twelve. Not counting Hadley."

Torn turned to Havelock. "I think we can hold this jail. If we take out the three downstairs, we've cut down the odds quite a bit."

"Hold the jail?" queried Branson.

"You've got a choice to make, Caleb," said Torn. "You can take your sister out of here or you can fight alongside us."

"This man is a murderer, Torn," Havelock objected. "You can't let him walk."

"I didn't kill that man on the train," said Branson. "Don't expect you'll believe this, but it was Cobb, not me, that done it."

"That's corral dust," snorted Havelock.

"Whatever we do, we better do it pronto," advised Armstrong. "We stand around here playing chin music much longer, we'll have hell to pay."

"Why are you helping us?" Torn asked Branson.

"Because you saved my sister's life. She came to a few hours ago. Told me if it hadn't been for you she'd be dead now. Then Hadley told me it was his doing, her coming here. He sent her a note telling her about me being brought here to stand trial. He was going to use her to try to break me out of jail." Branson shook his head. "I've ridden for Hadley a long time. used to look up to him. But he crossed the line with me when he thought to risk my sister's life. He shouldn't never have dragged her into this. I always tried to keep her out. She's all the family I got left." He shrugged. "I guess that doesn't make much sense to you."

"Yes, it does," said Torn. "And I believe you. You've still got that choice. You can make a run for it. If you do, you'll have a price on your head for the murder of that postal employee. Maybe you're telling the truth about that. Maybe not. A jury can decide. If you stay and fight with us, it'll be something in your favor."

Branson's eyes glittered behind the unruly yellow hair that had fallen forward over his face.

"I'm not sure Kate's in any condition to ride anyway. I'm with you, Judge. You've treated me fair. I reckon this will be my last chance to come clean. I'd like to do that—have a chance to start over. For Kate, mostly. Somehow I feel like I've let her down."

Torn checked the loads in the Colt Peacemaker. "Where is Kate?"

"The back room."

"Okay." Torn looked at Armstrong. "You and I will go down first."

"And I'll be watching you, mister," Havelock warned Branson. "One wrong move and you'll eat lead."

Branson's smile was shy, amiable. "I'm through making wrong moves, Marshal. This time I'm making the right move."

Torn's throat was dry. His heart was pumping strong and fast. He knew the signs; he was going into action. His hands were steady, his senses keen, his mind clear.

"Let's clean up Cass County," he said.

Armstrong grinned.

Torn went first, followed by the young deputy. He did not rush down the stairs, but walked normally, almost casually. The bushwhackers in the office were talking.

"Wish Hadley would hurry up with his breakfast," one was grousing. "I say we hang the men we're going to hang and get the hell out of town."

Another chuckled. "Relax, Cobb. It's not like you to bitch about free vittles."

Torn could see them now. The man named Cobb sat behind the desk, his feet propped up. A second man was perched on the corner of the desk, and the third was standing at the stove, pouring himself a cup of coffee.

It was the third man who looked up first.

It was just a glance—quickly followed by a double take flush with alarm. His mouth opened to yell a warning. He dropped the tin cup into which he was pouring steaming black java. The coffeepot clattered on the stove top, tipped over. The coffee hissed as it smothered the fire in the potbelly's innards, producing a cloud of steam. The bushwhacker reached for his side gun. Torn fired twice, jumped the last few steps, and landed in a crouch. The slugs slammed into the third bushwhacker, hurling him back against the wall. He slid to the floor, leaving a smear of blood.

The two outlaws at the desk reacted quickly. Each man got off a shot before Armstrong answered with a full choke blast from his scattergun. The double-aught picked one of the bushwhackers off his feet and threw him over the desk. Cobb spun as buckshot shredded his left arm. He got off another shot. Armstrong grunted, fell. Standing tall, icy calm, Torn took two steps forward, and with each step fired a shot. Both bullets struck Cobb, chest and throat, dropping him. His bootheels drummed the worn, blood-splattered floor planking a moment, and death rattled in his throat.

Torn walked over and checked both bushwhackers sprawled behind the desk, confirming that they were dead. He turned to find Branson at one of the windows, peering through the shutter gun slot. Havelock knelt beside Armstrong, whipped off his neckerchief, and applied it as a tourniquet on the deputy's leg, above the gunshot wound midway between hip and knee.

"How bad is it?" asked Torn.

"He'll pull through," said Havelock. "He's got grit. I should know; I've known him since he was small enough to trip over a cow track."

"Caleb!"

It was Kate, standing in the doorway to the back room.

Branson rushed to her. "You shouldn't be up, sis."

She scanned the room, shocked, and her gaze came to rest on Torn. He thought she looked relieved to see him unharmed. His next thought was that he might just be flattering himself.

He heard men shouting from the street, moved swiftly to the door, and dropped the crossbar.

"Branson," he snapped, "get your sister into the other room and watch the back door."

Kate stared curiously at her brother.

"I'm on the right side of the law for once, Kate," said Branson.

A bushwhacker's rifle was leaning against the wall near the door. Torn holstered the Colt and snatched up the long gun. Stepping to one of the windows, he peered through the gun slot. A half dozen outlaws, guns drawn, were converging on the jailhouse.

"Look lively, Marshal," he said, and poked the barrel of the rifle through the slot to shatter the window glass.

Havelock jumped to the other window. Torn started firing as fast as he could work the repeater's action. The men in the street scattered, shooting back, and gun thunder shattered the stillness of morning.

Just a quiet little town, thought Torn. . . .

CHAPTER 29

THE BUSHWHACKERS IN THE STREET CONCEN-
trated their fire on the windows of the stone jailhouse. Glass shattered; hot lead chunked into the
heavy wood of the shutters. Most of the outlaws
headed for cover, but two charged the jail. Havelock
stopped one dead in his tracks, but the other reached
the wall next to Torn's window. He shoved the barrel
of his pistol through the shutter gun slot. Torn struck
the barrel aside a second before the gun went off.
Dropping the empty repeater, he pulled the Colt
Peacemaker, stuck it through the gun slot, and fired
point-blank into the bushwhacker.

Torn peered through the slot in time to see Havelock bring down another longrider. The surviving
bushwhackers set up a blistering fire from the door
and windows of the mercantile across the street as

well as from the alleys on either side of the shebang.

Putting his back to the stone wall of the jail, Torn fed a fresh round into the Colt to replace the one empty shell. He'd learned it was a wise man who took every opportunity to fully load his weapons.

With this in mind, he checked the dead bushwhackers for .44 caliber bullets to fill the Winchester repeater, and found a box of center-fire cartridges in the pocket of one man's duster.

Back at his window, he reloaded the rifle, glanced across at Havelock.

"Better save your ammunition," he advised.

The marshal had been popping off at the bushwhackers, to no good effect as far as Torn could see.

"You like to tell people what to do, don't you, Judge?"

Torn grimaced. "I've been meaning to ask you something, Marshal. From the first it seemed like you had a bone you wanted to pick with me."

Havelock stopped shooting and gave Torn a long, less-than-friendly stare.

"I fought for the Union, Judge, as did my father and my younger brother. Both of them lost their lives, one at Shiloh, the other at Vicksburg. For years after the war a strong hate for any and all secesh ate at my guts. I still don't have much nice to say about anybody who fought for the Confederacy. Now, you I tried to give the benefit of the doubt. But it don't come easy, taking orders from an ex-Confederate. And if that creates a problem, Judge, well, just excuse the hell out of me, because I don't give a damn."

Scowling belligerently, he fired a couple more rounds through the gun slot, then ducked down to reload. A bushwhacker's bullet nicked splinters off the edge of the gun slot and shimmied across the room to thump into the back wall.

"Reckon we can hold 'em," said Havelock. "But I wish Wheeler would get his butt back here."

The shooting from across the street slacked off. Torn peered through his gun slot, wondering what Hadley was up to. If Branson's count was correct, Fourcade had five or six men left. They were cutting down the odds, and Torn felt somewhat encouraged by that, but he knew better than to underestimate Hadley Fourcade.

Three bushwhackers rushed the jailhouse, spread out across the street. Two men were firing pistols; the third carried two bottles with flaming rags sticking out of the necks. The two shooters aimed for the gun slots while the man with the firebombs aimed his throws at the door. Torn winged him as he let go of the first bottle. The bushwhacker staggered, let fly with the second bottle. Torn shot him down as glass shattered against the outer face of the door. Smoke began to seep through the cracks in the timber. The door was burning.

Havelock yelped and spun away from the window. A bullet had mangled the thumb of his right hand, and he dropped to his knees, hugging the injured hand against his body.

From the back room came the sound of splintering wood, followed by a rattle of gunfire. Torn turned and traded lead with the first man through the door to the sheriff's quarters. A bullet tugged at his frock coat. The outlaw pitched forward, gutshot.

Out in the street, a furious storm of gunfire was punctuated by the thunder of horses on the run. Torn heard Kate utter a small cry and headed for the back room. She was kneeling on the floor, Caleb's head in her lap. Branson was dead; this Torn could tell at a glance; his shirtfront was slick with blood. He'd given a good accounting of himself. Two bushwhackers were sprawled dead in the doorway.

Torn dragged the bodies out of the way, closed the shattered remains of the back door, and blocked it with a heavy trunk. He stood there a moment, trying to think of comforting words for Kate. In the end he took the easy way out, leaving her alone with her grief and returning to the front room.

The shooting outside had stopped. Torn peered through a gun slot and saw mounted men milling in the street. He recognized one of them.

U.S. Deputy Marshal Wheeler.

The front door of the jailhouse was burning; Torn kicked the crossbar out of its brackets, and a moment later Wheeler prodded the door open with the barrel of his long gun. The rifle swept the room. Then Wheeler saw Torn through the swirl of acrid smoke. The deputy flashed a grin and lowered the rifle.

"Well," Torn said, "you made it to the war on time."

Wheeler was looking around at the dead bushwhackers. "Barely."

As Wheeler tended to Havelock, Torn stepped out onto the boardwalk. Dead men were sprawled in the snow and slush of the street. He checked them all. Wheeler emerged from the jailhouse to meet him as he returned.

"Fourcade?" asked the deputy.

Torn grimly shook his head.

At Wheeler's gesture, four riders converged.

"Hadley Fourcade is still alive," said Wheeler. "Spread out and find him."

"Judge! Judge Torn!"

It was Mayor Armbruster, scuttling down the street, his game leg slowing him down. "Judge, Hadley's holed up in the hotel. He's got Odom under the gun. He's not trying to escape. He's waiting for you. Says you're to come alone. Said something about settling the account."

Torn nodded. "I'd say it's past time."

"I think we should all go in at once," said Wheeler. "He wouldn't stand a chance."

Torn was reloading his Colt Peacemaker.

"You stay out of this," he warned. "It's between me and Hadley."

CHAPTER

30

TORN FOUND HADLEY IN THE HOTEL BARROOM.
In Torn's opinion, a saloon by any other name was
still a saloon. This one was just a shade more stylish
than most. The ceiling was coffered, the walls were
covered with red damask, the camphene lamps
sported milk-glass shades, and the deal tables were
covered with green baize to match the green leather
upholstery of the chairs.

Hadley and Odom were the only two in the place,
sitting at a table in the back. The lawyer looked over
his shoulder at Torn as Torn came down the long
room. A sheen of perspiration covered Odom's face.
He was scared—as scared as a man could get short
of blubbering like a child.

"Let me go, Hadley," muttered Odom. "You have
no reason to harm me. This is the man you want."

"I told you once, Mr. Odom," said Torn. "You're not among gentlemen here. Hadley doesn't need a reason to kill you. I, on the other hand, have a reason. You're an accessory to the murder of Deputy United States Marshal Les Jennings."

Odom sucked in a breath, as though someone had just punched him in the belly.

"I had no choice, Judge. You have my word on that."

"Your word doesn't count for much."

"They . . . they would have harmed my wife if I hadn't helped them."

"You got a sudden case of cold feet, Lawyer Odom," drawled Hadley. "So I had to motivate you."

Fourcade sat with his back to the corner. On the table before him stood a half-empty bottle of Old Crow and the .44 Starr Army revolver.

"So what are you going to do with this man?" Torn asked him impatiently. "You going to kill him or let him go?"

Hadley made a dismissive gesture. "Oh, he can go. I don't need him anymore."

Chair legs screeched across the floor as Odom stood up in haste. As he scurried past, Torn reached out and gathered up a handful of sweat-soggy shirtfront.

"You'd better get yourself a fast horse or a good attorney, Mr. Odom."

Not a trace of color remained in Odom's face. Torn let him go with a contemptuous shove and turned his attention on Hadley as the lawyer hastened out of the barroom.

Fourcade was smiling, tracing the scar on his cheek with his finger.

"Lawyer Odom lacks commitment to the Cause," observed Hadley.

"You lie down with dogs, you get up with fleas," said Torn, sitting in the chair vacated by Odom. He put both hands on the table. "Why didn't you run, Hadley? You know how to run. I saw you run at Gettysburg."

"I'm here for the same reason you are." Hadley laughed, a harsh and unpleasant sound. "I knew you'd come alone. You're a fool, Clay. Still a gentleman. Still believing in that code of honor. Hell, you should have sent those lawmen in here with guns blazing. That would have been the end of me, and you could have ridden out of Harrisonville alive. As it is, I'm afraid you're bound for the local bone orchard."

"You're going to pay for my brother's death," said Torn. "And I'm the only one who can collect on that debt."

"Pistols at twenty paces?"

Moving slowly, Torn drew the Colt Peacemaker and set it on the table next to Hadley's .44 Starr.

"How about pistols at point-blank range?"

Hadley looked at the guns, then into Torn's steel-cast eyes. A slow grin curled one corner of his mouth.

"Can't miss at this range, can we, Clay?"

He grabbed for the Starr, rising from his chair. Torn scooped up the Colt and shoved the table into Hadley, throwing Fourcade off-balance. Hadley fell back into the corner, the Starr blazing. Instead of standing, Torn threw himself to the floor and rolled, shooting up through the overturned table. He emptied the Colt Peacemaker. Hadley pitched forward, shattering the table into so much kindling.

Moving the debris aside, Torn rolled Hadley over. He saw the blade reflecting the light of the camphene lamps and fell backward, twisting desperately away from the stroke. The saber-knife bit deep into his arm. Dispensing with the empty revolver, he picked up a table leg and swung it at Hadley's head with all his might as Hadley started to get up. Blood spewed out of Hadley's nose and mouth as he corkscrewed and fell.

This time he fell on the blade of the saber-knife.

Clutching his arm, hot blood streaming through his fingers, Torn looked down at Hadley as Fourcade breathed his last.

And as Hadley died, he grinned crookedly at Torn.

"I'll be waiting for you in hell, Clay. . . ."

Torn pulled the saber-knife out of Fourcade's unmoving chest, wiped the blade clean on Hadley's clothes, and left the barroom.

Wheeler was waiting for him out on the hotel boardwalk.

"Is it over?" asked the deputy.

Torn looked over his shoulder. He had an eerie feeling, a tingling at the base of his spine. He half expected to see Hadley Fourcade standing there bloody and grinning.

"I hope so," Torn said, and headed across the muddy street toward the jailhouse.

*   *   *

A few days later Torn stopped by the jailhouse to say his so-longs to Frank Havelock. The marshal was standing in the sun slanting under the boardwalk roof. It was a cold but sunny day. Harrisonville bustled with activity. Havelock was watching the goings-on with a cynical eye.

"Came to say good-bye, Marshal," said Torn.

Havelock gave him a long look, then stuck out his bandaged right hand. The bushwhacker's bullet had sheared the thumb off at the joint. Torn took the proffered hand gingerly, shook it.

"Where you headed, Judge?"

"Jefferson City. I'm going to see Kate Branson safely home."

"Tell her I'm sorry about her brother."

Torn smiled. "You're not going soft on me, are you, Marshal?"

Havelock scowled. "Don't start with me, Torn."

"I hate to admit it," said Torn, tongue-in-cheek, "but you're a good man, Marshal. One to ride the river with."

"I was going to say the same thing about you, Judge, except I was afraid I'd choke on the words."

They both grinned.

"Maybe we'll work together again sometime."

"You never know," allowed Havelock. "But if we do, I'll give the orders, and you can get all shot to hell and gone. Deal?"

Torn and Kate rode north out of Harrisonville, he on the dun gelding, she on a rented horse; because of the snow, repair on the railroad had been delayed.

They paused at the cemetery a quarter mile out of town. Kate paid her last respects to Caleb. When she was finished, she found Torn standing grim-faced over Hadley Fourcade's grave. Hadley's name had been carved into the simple wooden cross; later someone had etched the letters CSA after the name.

"You knew him during the war?" she asked. "Caleb said you and Hadley served together."

Torn nodded. "We were in the same regiment."

"What happened between you?"

"It's a long story." Torn smiled at her. "Let's just say we had a little misunderstanding."

They headed for their horses and the road out of Cass County.